The Dog Who Would Not Smile

Stephen Bly

CROSSWAY BOOKS • WHEATON, ILLINOIS
A DIVISION OF GOOD NEWS PUBLISHERS

Cover illustration: David Yorke

Banner: Keith Stubblefield

First printing, 1992

Printed in the United States of America

For a list of other books by Stephen Bly or information regarding
speaking engagements, write: Stephen Bly, Winchester, ID 83555.

Library of Congress Cataloging-in-Publication Data
Bly, Stephen, 1944-
    The dog who would not smile / Stephen Bly.
      p.   cm.
    Summary: When his parents are not in the frontier town where he
expected to meet them, twelve-year-old Nathan sets out to find them,
encountering prospectors, Indians, outlaws, and a loyal dog along the
way.
    [1. West (U.S.)—Fiction. 2. Frontier and pioneer life—Fiction.
3. Dogs—Fiction.] I. Title.
PZ7.B6275Do 1992   [Fic]—dc20   91-34250
ISBN 0-89107-656-5

00		99		98		97		96		95		
15	14	13	12	11	10	9	8	7	6	5	4	

The Dog Who Would Not Smile

*For
Aaron and his
friends*

1

Nathan felt the stagecoach hit something hard and suddenly jerk to the left. Then it settled down to a steady bounce.

Why do grown-ups talk about us as if we weren't listening? he grumbled under his breath. For a moment voices faded in the rattle of the ride.

Then the man spoke again, "Looks like your boy's gone to sleep, ma'am."

"Well, he doesn't belong to me!" The woman's voice sounded high and shrill. "I thought he was yours."

"Mine?" the man growled.

"He entered the coach with you." She spoke the last word with authority.

"Now if I recall correctly, we all climbed aboard the stage at Battle Mountain Station," he drawled.

Even without opening his eyes, Nathan figured the man was surely from Texas.

The lady sighed.

Then the man cleared his throat. "It's not right to send a child off by hisself in country like this."

"It certainly isn't." The woman's crisp reply brought the discussion to a sudden close.

Nathan Riggins kept his smoky blue eyes closed. Awake, he'd have to explain why a twelve-year-old, ninety-pound boy was riding the stagecoach through northern Nevada alone. Asleep, he would be asked no questions.

It seemed like years since he had sat on the front porch of his grandfather's Indiana farm. Everything was supposed to have gotten better after the war. Once Nathan's dad came home, life was to be perfect again. But all of that seemed so long ago, like something out of a dream.

The stage lurched forward and tossed Nathan to the rear. He wanted to scream. Long, hot, dusty, and boring. The whole trip had been that way. Nathan hadn't spoken to anyone but ticket agents and train conductors. He found himself in an adult world, where most folks looked right over the top of him, both with their eyes and their words.

Nobody ever called Nathan shy back home. *But everything out here is so . . . foreign! At least this part will be over soon.*

In Willow Creek Nathan would be with his mom and dad again. He hadn't seen them in months. It would be a big, happy party!

Of course, he dreaded telling them about the smallpox epidemic, about Grandma and Grandpa dying. And he knew his mother would be angry that he couldn't get along with Uncle Jed. *At least they have my letter.*

Nathan promised himself that he would never take another stagecoach ride. He was either freezing or roasting, and always bouncing. *A stagecoach trip is like a toothache*, he thought grimly.

"Pain before pleasure," Grandpa used to tell him. "Before you eat watermelon, you've got to work the garden."

Beads of sweat dripped off Nathan's forehead, but he didn't bother wiping. He knew it would only smear the road dust that clung to his body. *Nobody cares what I look like anyway.*

Some coins jingled in his bouncing coat pocket, and he reviewed his plan. *I'll buy Mom a new hat and a little folding knife for Dad.* Nathan amazed even himself that he had traveled across the country and still had $3.50 to spare.

He pushed up the front edge on his round-brimmed, brown felt hat and barely opened one eye to examine the other passengers.

Sitting next to him, but leaning against the far side of the coach, was the woman with the high voice. Black lace trimmed the cuffs and high collar of her long dark dress. She clutched a large green handbag in her lap. Her hat tilted toward her right ear, and her frown looked like it was painted on her face. *She must be a schoolteacher*, he decided. For the first time in weeks, he thought about school. He would certainly miss Bradford and Nelson, and maybe even Melissa, although she could be a real bother at times.

The man sitting across from him wore a tall black hat that looked very worn. His coat sleeves were too short, and the buttons had long since disappeared.

Nathan noticed a black-handled revolver tucked into the man's belt. The gun especially caught his eye because of the gold trigger.

Nathan didn't bother looking out the window. For several days the landscape had been the same—rolling, treeless mountains and high desert basin covered with sagebrush. His head slapped against the stage wall, and the woman gasped as they rounded a corner. Back home, everyone said that the West was full of bears, snakes, and Indians. So far, Nathan had seen none of these. He thought he had seen an Indian at a depot in Wyoming, but he wasn't sure. *Mainly, the West is full of nothing.*

The stage slowed to enter a settlement, and Nathan sat up. Most of the structures seemed to be tents scattered about in no apparent order. One wood building had two stories. A big sign above the second floor proclaimed: "Galena Store: Outfits Big & Small."

When the stage stopped, the lady and then the gentleman climbed out. Nathan stayed put. He had no one to see and nowhere to go. But he hung his head out the stage door window and stared down the street. A cloud of dust hovered overhead as the community hustled with activity. Supply wagons, lined four deep, unloaded at the Galena Store. The wooden sidewalks glared, unpainted and not yet weathered. *Everything here is so rough and bare*, he thought. *Just the basics.*

Nathan's eye followed a young girl carrying a heavy bucket of water across the street to a tent that posted a handwritten sign: "Walker's Haircuts & Dentistry." Even though the wooden buildings and tents came in different shapes, and most were new, the layer of clay-red dust made them all blend together. Nathan pulled off his hat and fanned his face. "It just can't be much longer," he rasped to himself, clearing the dust out of his throat.

"You might as well step out, son."

Nathan spun his head around to see Mr. Mallory, the stagecoach driver, standing beside a short man wearing glasses, who was tugging to loosen his black bow tie.

"Son, Henry has word from our boss that we are supposed to drop the run up to Willow Creek. We won't be going up there."

"But you can't do that! I paid for a ticket clear to Willow Creek," Nathan protested.

The man called Henry responded, "Well, young man, I'm certainly sorry. But they shut down Willow Creek two weeks ago. We ran a mail stage up there Friday, but we took no passengers and brought none back. Everyone is gone."

"Gone? A whole town gone?" Nathan shouted.

"I'm afraid so," the station agent added.

Nathan fought back rising fear and anger. "A town is a town! They don't just come and go like a circus!"

Mr. Mallory explained, "It happens all the time out here whenever the gold and silver is gone. Most all the folks hurried to a place called Jersey. Rumor has it that the gold strike's big there. They want me to run the stage on down to Jersey. You're welcome to ride along."

"But," Nathan protested, "my parents are waiting for me at Willow Creek!"

Henry pulled an engraved, gold-cased watch out of

his vest pocket. "Well, Mallory's got a full load of passengers to roll out of here in less than one-half hour. You be here at the stage, and I'll let you ride up on top."

"From what I hear, son, there's not even a dog left at Willow Creek," Mallory added. "You'll have better luck finding your folks in Jersey, or Austin, or even Lander Hill."

"You don't understand," Nathan shouted. "I sent them a letter and everything. I mean, they will be expecting me to show up. They won't move without me. I'm their son!"

Mallory banged the dust off his trousers with his hat. "Suit yourself, boy. Maybe you can find a wagon headed for Willow Creek and ride along. But I doubt if there is anybody on earth who's going up there now."

The two men drifted inside the stage office, and Nathan walked around to the back of the stagecoach and unfastened his satchel. *Lord, this isn't fair. Nobody told me that whole towns move!*

He banged the small suitcase down on the wooden sidewalk, and his eyes searched the street. Teamsters shouted from their wagons; men on horseback crowded the street; men carrying supplies on their backs scurried by.

The girl he had seen carrying the water walked over and stared down at his feet.

"Yeah, what do you want?" Nathan scolded.

"Where did you get them shoes?" she asked.

"In Chicago. They're the latest style. I don't suppose you've ever been to Chicago," he boasted.

"I've been to Virginia City three times," she shot

back. "And I ain't never seen shoes like those." She started to walk away. Nathan suddenly regretted being rude to the only person his age he'd talked to for more than a month.

"Hey, wait! Listen, I need to get to Willow Creek. Where can I get a ride?" he asked.

"Ain't nobody up there. Ain't nobody going up there." She brushed the front of her long dress and turned to scoot back across the street.

For the first time, Nathan noticed her bare feet. "Well, my mother and father are there! And I'm going there!" he shouted.

His confidence faded the minute the girl was out of sight. It was just another town full of strangers. Finally, he waited in line to talk to one of the clerks at the Galena Store about hitching a ride on a freight wagon.

"Willow Creek? Son, that town is gone! Now trot on out of here. I've no time for chats."

Nathan crossed the street and talked to a man leaning against an empty corral where a sign said: "Horses for Sale or Trade." The answer was the same. Gathering up as much courage as he could, he walked up to a well-dressed stranger and asked him to help. The man ignored him completely.

Nathan was still hurrying about looking for a ride to Willow Creek when the stage rolled out for Jersey. The only person that would talk to him was an old man sitting on the wooden bench in front of the Welsh Miners' Hall.

"So you're wanting to go to Willow Creek?" He squinted and shaded his eyes with his sun-tanned hand.

"I can't find a ride. Why is everyone so rude?"

"Gold." The old man grabbed Nathan by the shoulder and stuck his face up close. "It drives them all crazy."

Startled by the sudden move and the smell of the man, Nathan pulled back. "Eh, just how far is it to Willow Creek anyway?" he asked.

"Well, you go back down Duck Creek a mile or so and then slant off to the left until you come to a crossroad. At that point take a left and start climbing uphill. It's maybe fifteen more miles."

"More than fifteen miles?" Nathan groaned.

"Yep."

"But," Nathan grumbled, "I couldn't walk that far before dark."

The old man shook his head. "Nope, I don't reckon you could. Maybe you should buy yourself a horse."

"How much do they cost?"

"Twenty, twenty-five dollars." He shrugged. "Not including the saddle."

"Well, I can't afford that," Nathan complained.

The old man once again stuck his nose in Nathan's face. "Don't matter, there ain't none left to sell anyway."

Nathan jumped to his feet. "Well, I'm going to walk then."

"I guess you could hike over Big Belle Mountain," the old man suggested.

"Where's that?" Nathan quizzed.

"See that mountain over there? Sort of looks like a little tower in the middle? Well, that's Big Belle. From up on top, you can look down and see Willow Creek. It would cut the trip to about twelve miles, but there's no trail that way."

"I could get there before dark!" Nathan crowed.

"Maybe, maybe not. It's a tough, hot climb this time of the year. Take my advice," the old man added, "pack some extra water. Ain't no springs on Big Belle."

"Er, are there any mountain lions up there?" Nathan asked.

The old man slapped his knee and laughed. "No lions, tigers, or elephants!"

Nathan thought about the rumors he had heard. "How about snakes and Indians?"

"Well, that's another story. I doubt if you'll see either one, but you never can tell. It's a pretty safe trip except for the heat, like I said."

Nathan started to walk across the street. Then he turned back to the old man. "Is Willow Creek really empty?" he asked.

"Nah, Mrs. Fromly will still be there. Probably Earl Thunder, too. I haven't seen him pass through here yet."

"And my parents," Nathan added.

He bought a canteen at the store and filled it full of pump water. Then he bought several sticks of beef jerky and one peppermint candy. He stuffed all of his purchases in his satchel and hiked out of town towards Big Belle Mountain.

For the first time all day, Nathan allowed himself to relax. "Twelve miles won't be all that bad," he mumbled aloud as he pushed past some sagebrush. "I once hiked eight miles to the county fair with Bradford Oakes."

The memory of a hike down a tree-lined Indiana lane only made the journey here seem more harsh. A hot summer wind blasted across the high desert mountains, and the sand stung his face. Nathan had hiked no more than a mile when he tossed down his suitcase and rested beside a tall gray, strong-smelling sage. His feet burned from the heat of his shoes, and he remembered the girl back in town. "If she can go barefoot, so can I," he insisted to the empty desert. But after a dozen painful hops on the hot sand, he collapsed and carefully tucked his swollen feet back into the tight shoes.

Nathan trudged along until he finally made it to the base of the mountain. He could look back down the sloping basin and see Galena in the distance. His knees and legs were starting to ache from walking through the loose sand and dirt. Nathan pulled out a piece of jerky and scrambled higher. He leaned against the brisk wind and tried to keep his chapped lips shut tight against the blowing sand.

Looking back over his shoulder, Nathan came to a sudden stop.

Someone or something is following me!

A chill ran down his back. His arms tingled.

It's a wolf! I know it's a wolf. I've seen their pictures!

He grabbed up a pointed stick.

He kept climbing the mountain with one eye on the animal. Whenever he stopped for a rest, it stopped. When he ran, the animal ran. But it never came any closer to

Nathan. After about an hour, the animal disappeared from sight, which both relieved and worried Nathan.

But he had worse problems. Blisters on his feet rubbed hard against the leather shoes. He dreamed of a cool pond to soak his feet in and a soft, smooth pair of shoes.

Nathan pulled himself up on some large boulders that had been dug out of the mountainside and lay scattered in a semicircle around a fairly deep pit. He plopped down and gulped water from his canteen. The bright orange sun had already begun to rest on the mountains behind him.

I'm going to have to spend a night out here on this mountain!

He peeled his shoes off again and inspected his feet. The puffy skin bled where the blisters had rubbed raw. Grabbing an old shirt out of his leather case, he ripped it into strips and bandaged his sores. Nathan shoved his shoes back on and plodded once more up Big Belle.

This is really dumb! Who do I think I am? I'm just a boy. I shouldn't be out here in the middle of nowhere!

By the time he reached the crest of the mountain, it was so dark he could not even see where Willow Creek was. Though his heart pushed him to go on, his body gave out.

He circled a pile of rocks, mumbling to himself. "I can't hike after dark. I can't stay up here alone. But I can't go back."

Lord, if this is a really bad dream . . . well, this would be a good time to wake.

In the far distance he thought he heard a wolf howl. He decided to wait the night out against some rocks. He scrounged a few sticks to make a small fire. In the approaching darkness, he could not see a tree anywhere.

He saved one piece of jerky for breakfast and drank all but a couple swallows of his water. Then he sucked on the peppermint stick as he leaned back. The night air chilled him, but he enjoyed its clean taste, free from the constant cloud of dust on the endless stagecoach ride. First one star, then another blinked in the sky. The low sage and the occasional rock blended in the blackness of the night, limiting his view to the edges of the little fire.

Nathan had not once, even in the past few weeks, felt so alone. Indiana was far away. His parents were nowhere in sight. Home, school, church, friends—even Galena, Nevada, felt distant.

Lord, it's me, Nathan T. Riggins. I'm way out here, and I hope You're watching. I know there aren't many people out here, but the ones that are here are important . . . sort of.

He reached down for a stick and stirred the fire. He fumbled in his satchel for his hunting knife. Then he rolled up his overcoat into a pillow. Nathan laid the knife within arm's reach.

Though the small fire warmed him, he shivered as he imagined that someone, or something, might be waiting just outside its light.

2

*T*he dream didn't scare Nathan.

It just wore him out.

All night long he had walked behind his grandfather's wagon, tossing rocks out of Indiana bottom land. He woke up tired.

A cool morning breeze now rubbed against his cheeks and lifted his eyelids. He half expected to see his grandfather standing there, urging him to continue.

With the polished buck-horn handle of the hunting knife gripped tightly in his right hand, he sat up quickly and looked around. The dream had confused him.

Nevada! Mom and Dad!

For some reason Nathan remembered the time he and Bradford Oakes slept all night on a raft and ended up drifting six miles downstream. They thought they had been kidnapped by river pirates until Bradford's dad came looking for them.

That's the worst whippin' I ever got.

Nathan scrounged up a few more sticks of wood and rebuilt the fire to warm his hands.

If Oakes were here, he'd know what to do. I told him we'd probably find gold and get rich, but he just laughed and said he'd stay back in Indiana and protect Melissa.

"If there's anyone in the world who doesn't need protecting, it's her! Bradford, you're crazy," he called out to the wind.

Then Nathan turned to a nearby sagebrush and spoke to it as if it were his friend.

"Now look, Oakes, I've got a bit of trouble here. See that town way down there? Where the white reflections are? Well, that's Galena. And over here, see those buildings next to that big tin barn, or factory, or whatever? Well, that's supposed to be Willow Creek, and that's where my parents are waiting for me. I'm going to find them today. I don't plan on spending one more night alone. It's only a few miles. I'm going to grab my stuff, hike down there, and, and . . .

"I'm going to stop talking to myself."

Nathan climbed the boulder that had served as a backdrop for his camp and scanned the north. Barren mountain ridges unfolded in silent regiments of canyons and cliffs. Down the steep slope of Big Belle, Willow Creek seemed only a few miles away in the clear mountain air. But Nathan suspected it was further. A chill rolled up his back as he stared at the distant outline of the town. He was anxious to finally come face to face with his parents. And yet there was an ache of fear in his stomach. Would they be there?

He stuffed his belongings back into his suitcase, grabbed it up without fastening it, and spilled most of the contents on the ground. As he scooped them up, he stopped abruptly and fell to his knees to examine the fresh tracks ahead of him.

That wolf! He was here!

The dirt was smooth next to a small sage just across from where Nathan had slept. He followed the track for only a moment as it zigzagged down the mountain.

It had spent the night right here!

Fumbling with his suitcase once more, he pulled out his hunting knife and turned toward Willow Creek.

"I'll need to hit him with something big, like a rock. Yeah, I'll hit him with a rock. Then I'll grab him and stab him with my knife. Of course, I'll have to do it quick. They say wounded animals are more dangerous."

His voice faded into a whisper. The brave words hid his rising fear.

Nathan's feet felt stronger as he began the descent. He rushed halfway down Big Belle, finally stopping to catch his breath. Tossing his suitcase to the ground, he leaned against a lone boulder, the only thing standing out from the smooth high basin landscape.

Pulling his hat low and squinting his eyes, Nathan scanned the red-layered sandstone mountainside. The clear, blue Nevada sky and the stark silence made Nathan feel absolutely alone. Then near a cluster of sage he spied the beast. Their eyes met.

After a long moment, Nathan blurted, "I know you know that I know you're following me. Well, don't mess with me. I've got a knife! And my dad's in Willow Creek, and he's got a gun. You get too close to me, and he'll blow your head off!" Nathan waved the knife, then turned, and hurried down the mountain.

His feet felt raw and hot again, and that familiar pain began shooting up both legs. For the longest time Willow Creek didn't seem to be getting any closer. His mouth parched, his lips chapped, Nathan finally limped onto a dusty wagon road.

The dream of a grand meeting with his parents gave way to the reality and pain of the day. Nathan knew for a fact that when he found them, he would just break down and cry.

A half-mile from Willow Creek, he still could not see any signs of life, but once his feet began tracing the wagon rut, he forgot about looking back for the wolf.

The trail into town wound through the dig holes of disappointed prospectors. To Nathan, it looked like a village of giant prairie dogs. The brown earth blended into reds, yellows, and whites as it was scooped and piled on the slopes of the rolling mountains. Every inch of ground looked as if it had been dug up and examined. Tunnel shafts had been blasted out of mountainsides. Broken and rusted mining equipment cluttered the landscape.

With a rush of energy, Nathan sprinted the last hundred yards, forgetting about his blistered feet, tired muscles, and the stalking animal. Long stage rides, towns full of strangers, and embarrassing scenes lost their grip on his mind.

"I made it!" he shouted. "Willow Creek, Nevada, Nathan T. Riggins is here! I did it!"

His yell was the only sound he heard.

Empty.

Almost like a dream—the kind Nathan used to have. He would dream he woke up, and everyone he knew was gone, and he didn't know where they went.

Willow Creek, Nevada.

Just one wide dusty street with a double row of unpainted wooden buildings and sidewalks facing each other like toy soldiers that would never go into battle. But there was no blue and gray . . . just a rich coat of red dirt caked on everything in sight.

It's like going to school on a Saturday. Everything's in place but the people! Between the street and the mountains Nathan could see scattered remains of tents and half-built structures.

But not a song.

Not a shout.

Not a baby's cry.

Not a dog's bark.

Not a mother yelling at her children.

Nothing.

Nathan walked down the south side of the street. One building had hooks where a sign had hung over the door. All the building's windows, casings, and doors had been removed. Inside was an empty shell of a room that sported a freshly painted sign on the wall: "No Spitting Allowed."

Next door stood a building fully furnished. A small dust-covered couch lined the entry way, and a benchless piano filled the center of the parlor. Musty pictures tilted on the walls. Some newspapers were stacked in the corner.

"Hey, is anybody home?" he yelled.

The words seemed to be sucked up into the fading red wallpaper.

Nathan thought the noise of his own shoes on the wooden sidewalk seemed terribly loud . . . and lonesome.

Another building was completely boarded up, and a note was scribbled on the front door: "Charles, we've gone to the Jersey district."

Nathan read the note over and over. He hurt really bad inside. He searched for some hope, some sign that his parents were still in town.

At the end of the street, Nathan saw a structure that was really only half of a building. The wooden walls went up about four feet, with a big white tent forming the top half of the room. Inside, he found long tables and benches. In the back was a kitchen behind some blankets that had been strung across a rope in the dining hall. Hundred-pound sacks of flour lay ripped open in one corner. Little black bugs swarmed over the white powder on the floor.

Nathan crossed the street and pushed his way into another building.

"Hey, where is everyone?" he called out through the doors of a place named The Three Queens. He spotted several bullet holes in the wall and jumped as a rat ran across the bare floor. He quickly backed out.

At the Willow Creek Mercantile, Nathan stepped through the window. This building, like many of the others, had all the window glass and frames removed. Wooden shelves still lined one wall, but otherwise the place was stripped. He noticed several broken boxes standing guard around a blackened spot on the floor that had once been the home to a wood stove.

He felt hungry, thirsty, and very alone. Sitting down on one of the broken boxes, he looked around at the empty, musty room. He didn't want to cry. Not yet. For weeks his daily survival had rested on the fact that one day he would stand on these streets of Willow Creek and run into his parents' arms.

Tears, or something that felt like tears, began to drip from his eyes.

He had no other plan. This had been his only goal.

I don't know what to do. I don't want to figure out what to do. Lord, I'm tired of all this. I'm too young for this! God, it's not fair. You promised to be with me wherever I went, but here I am, all alone!

After a few minutes of watching his tears splash tiny, muddy puddles on the floor, Nathan took a deep breath, stood to his feet, and declared, "I'm starved!" Searching every square inch of the building, he spotted something brown behind one of the standing shelves.

"It might be an old loaf of bread!"

By placing his feet against the wall and pressing both hands on the shelves, he pried the case away and grabbed the hidden object. It turned out to be a pair of knee-high beaded deerhide moccasins.

"Oh, great, I wanted something to eat, and all I find—"

Nathan sat down on the floor and pulled off his store-bought shoes, carefully unwrapping the rags and inspecting each foot. Slowly he slipped on the moccasins and tucked his pants inside as he laced them up. There was a turquoise and coral pattern halfway up the side of each moccasin.

This is the only good thing that's happened to me in weeks!

He was still sitting on the floor admiring his new footwear when he heard a pounding noise and a crash from the rear of the building.

"Who's out there?" Nathan yelled by instinct as he ran for the rear of the building. He was still yelling when he swung open the back door.

Towering over him on its hind feet was a snarling black bear wearing something that looked like a yellow bonnet.

Nathan wanted to scream.

His mouth was open, yet no sound came out.

Nathan wanted to turn quickly and run.

But his feet felt nailed to the floor.

Nathan wanted to cry.

Yet even his tears were frozen with fear.

Suddenly, he heard another growl and a snap from the side of the building. Both he and the bear jerked around to see an animal flying through the air at the back side of the bear. Returning to all fours, the bear retreated behind some outbuildings.

Nathan took a deep breath and wiped the cold sweat from his forehead.

It's that wolf! It jumped the bear!

The animals roared up the hill toward a large tin-roofed building that looked like it was built in layers. Nathan watched as the bear burst through a gate toward the entrance of the building. The other animal halted, prowled a few steps, and then sat down to guard the bear.

"You two just about scared the breakfast out of Mrs. Fromly."

The sudden sound of human speech sent goose bumps down Nathan's back. He spun around to see a tall, bearded man, his arms hanging over the barrel and stock of a shotgun slung straight across his shoulders.

"Who are you?" Nathan blurted out.

"Guess I scared you a bit," he laughed. "I suppose you thought this town was empty. I'm Earl Thunder." He took his arms off the shotgun and lowered it. "Who are you?"

"Nathan T. Riggins from Indiana, and I'm looking for my parents, David and Adele Riggins. Have you seen them?" Nathan spat out the words quickly and gasped for a breath of air like a person who has been swimming underwater for a long time.

"Well, Nathan T. Riggins from Indiana, just relax a bit. Don't guess I know your folks. If they were in Willow Creek, they aren't here now. I suppose they saddled up for Jersey, like the others."

"Aren't there any people in town? My parents wouldn't go off and leave me. They knew that I was on my way." Nathan was startled to hear his voice sounding so hurried and high-pitched, out of control.

"Sorry, son. Look around if you like. But Tuesday McReynolds left town last week, and he was the last. He

27

had been laid up with a fever and couldn't go on with the others. There's no one around these parts but Mrs. Fromly and me."

Nathan took a deep breath. "Who's this Mrs. Fromly? Maybe she knows my parents."

"Now that might be. But she don't talk much." Mr. Thunder chuckled.

Nathan looked up at the big man. "Well, where is she? I'll ask her."

"You and your dog chased her into the stamp mill."

"The bear? Mrs. Fromly is a bear?" Nathan shook his head in disbelief.

"Sure is. Tennessee Martin brought her down when she was a cub. I guess you'd call her the town mascot."

"But the hat?" Nathan questioned. "Why does she wear that?"

"One time she got into some fresh pies at the hotel, and the cook threw a hatchet at her. It just pealed off the hide on top of her head, and for several months we had a bald bear. Then Tennessee tied that bonnet on her so she wouldn't get sunburned, and she's worn it ever since. Looks strange, doesn't it?"

"Yeah. Is she dangerous?"

Earl Thunder grinned. "Only if you're holding food and she's hungry. What's your dog's name?"

"Dog? You mean that . . . wolf?" Nathan pointed.

"Wolf? Son, he may be a scraggly mutt. He may even have a touch of coyote, but for sure, he's no wolf. Look how that left ear flops down, and look at the color of the eyes. Anyway, I know he's your dog. I spied him following you all the way into town."

"Well," Nathan added, "he's not my dog. He just hung around my campfire last night, that's all."

"He might not belong to you, but you belong to him. He proved that when he dove at Mrs. Fromly."

Nathan shoved back his hat. "I belong to him?"

"What makes you think humans are the only ones who choose to have other creatures for friends? This dog has decided that you and him ought to be pals. He doesn't seem to care what you think of the arrangement."

"A wild dog? What kind of friend is that?" Nathan questioned.

"A better one than some men I've known. Out here a fella needs plenty of friends, even the kinds with hair and fur."

"I've got enough problems without having to take care of a dog," Nathan protested.

Earl Thunder started to approach the dog, who growled and circled around toward Nathan. "Sizing up that mutt, I'd say you won't have to feed him much, and you sure won't have to protect him."

"You don't understand," Nathan said. "I've traveled across this country by myself to meet my parents, and all I find in Willow Creek is a lousy, half-starved dog!"

"Well," Mr. Thunder replied, "it doesn't sound like he's getting much in the bargain either."

3

I don't believe this!" Nathan moaned. "It's like a bad dream that never ends. Look, I've got to find my parents. You don't happen to be going to this place, eh, Jersey, do you?"

"Afraid not. Earl Thunder never leaves a good claim. There's a lot more gold and silver up here, but those people didn't want to take the time to dig it out. They'll be back some day, and I'll own all of it."

"Do you have a horse I can borrow? I don't have any money, but my dad will pay you back. My word is good," Nathan pleaded.

"Well, son, I believe you. But all I've got is a lame mule that won't do you any good for a month." Mr. Thunder scratched his shoulder. "The only way out is to hike back to Galena and catch a ride. I suppose you can find your way back?"

"Sure, climb over Big Belle, right?" Nathan sighed.

"If you don't mind rattlesnakes and aren't thirsty. But the best fresh water around is at Trout Creek at the bottom of Copper Canyon. Head due east. It's just a little trot off the trail," the man replied.

"Rattlesnakes? I hiked over a mountain full of rattlesnakes?"

As the old man rambled on, Nathan tried to determine if he were extremely sun-tanned or just caked with dirt. "I didn't say it was full of snakes. But there's enough up there for a man to have a mighty fine Thanksgivin' dinner."

"You eat snakes!" Nathan gagged.

"A hungry man ain't all that particular," Mr. Thunder shrugged.

Nathan pulled off his hat and ran his fingers through his greasy hair. "Well, I can't believe my parents went off without me. I sent them a letter."

"Letter?" Earl Thunder waved his shotgun like a pointing stick toward the main street. "The stage brought in a bag of mail last week. But there was no one left here to sort it out. Ain't that strange? They deliver the mail to an empty town."

"Where's the post office?" Nathan quizzed.

"That stubby-looking building with the flat roof down at the end of the street. It used to have a big sign out front," Thunder offered.

Nathan shuffled toward the street with his hands shoved deep in his pockets. "How can a whole town just pack up and move?"

"Things happen quick in a boom town. Everyone's afraid the other guy will beat him to the new diggin's." He looked Nathan over up and down. "Say, are you hungry?"

"I'm starved!" Nathan exploded. Then he froze in

his tracks and turned toward the smiling Earl Thunder. "Eh, just what, exactly, do you have to eat?"

"Well, how about a little Willow Creek surprise? I'll dig around in the cook shack over by the mine, and if I come up with anything tasty that's worth eatin', it'll be a surprise," Thunder reported.

Nathan shuffled down the street trying to figure what kind of pan you have to use to cook a snake. He found the combination stage and post office without trouble. It was the only building that seemed to have escaped the exodus untouched. As he sprawled on the floor and dug through the letters and packages, he noticed that the warped boards on the wall allowed narrow streams of sunlight to shine through.

He sorted the mail slowly, hesitating out of fear. He read each name out loud, "My Dearest Billy Tewell," "Mr. A. T. Courtney," "Nelson O'Riley, Jr.," "Rosie McClelland and girls," "Marshall Steve Anson," "Buster Bailey," "Swifty Tucker . . ."

He had scattered most of the mail when he spotted his own handwriting: "Mr. & Mrs. David Riggins." Nathan crunched the letter in his clenched fist, then unfolded it, and stared at it again.

I mailed this almost two months ago. It's just now getting here? They promised it would only take two weeks to deliver.

Nathan kicked at the other mail in disgust as he left the office.

They could have left Willow Creek last winter! Maybe they wrote to me, and I was gone before the letter got there. Maybe they moved to California. Maybe they are on their way back to Indiana.

He crammed the unopened letter into his pocket and stalked back to find Mr. Thunder. Out of the corner of his eye Nathan spied the dog trailing behind him. Before he rounded the alley, he caught a whiff of smoke from a fire and the smell of meat frying.

"Hey, I found my letter!" Nathan shouted. "No wonder my folks weren't here to meet me. They didn't know I was coming. I guess they did move down to Jersey."

Nathan was not nearly as sad as he thought he would be. Now he knew why his parents were gone.

"Hope you like fried bread and salt pork. That's about all there is," Mr. Thunder replied.

"Is there plenty?" Nathan questioned.

"Well, there's a couple sacks of flour that the bugs haven't spoiled. Just how hungry are you?"

"Could I take some food with me?" Nathan explained.

Earl Thunder laughed loud and deep. "By all means. I'll fry you up an extra mess. I figure there's enough here to last a month for you, me, Mrs. Fromly, and that mutt of yours."

"He's not my dog, honest!" Nathan protested.

The tall, muscular man pulled a big wooden spoon out of the frying pan and pointed it at the dog. "Whatever you say. But I fixed him a pan of scrappings, and still he won't come within twenty yards of me. Why don't you feed him. I think he could use some beefin' up."

"Yeah, I guess I should thank him for helping me with the bear. Did you notice that he looks sad?"

Nathan approached the dog carrying a broken bucket half full of pork rinds.

"Well, the way you treat him, it's no wonder." Mr. Thunder flipped the fried bread as it sizzled in the pan.

As Nathan approached the two-and-a-half-foot-tall gray and white dog, the animal scooted back a few steps, tucked its ears down, and slung its head low, just waiting. It moved neither its head nor its tail. When Nathan set the bucket down and turned to leave, the dog trotted up to the food and began to gobble its contents. Nathan noticed for the first time that one of the dog's eyes was white.

Earl Thunder grabbed one bowl of scraps and hiked up the hill toward the big metal building. Nathan watched as he set the food down in the doorway and whistled. Before he had gotten back to the stove, out poked a yellow-bonneted bear head. Mrs. Fromly promptly poured everything into the dirt and licked the bowl.

After they had eaten, Nathan took a deep breath and sighed. "Things aren't going like I planned. All of this seemed a lot easier back home in Indiana."

"Well, son, you're learnin' all about providence. It happens to all of us sooner or later."

Nathan walked over to the fire and loaded up another plateful. "What do you mean, providence?"

Earl Thunder pushed his hat back and smiled. "There are just some trails in life you got to ride alone.

That's all." He wiped his mouth on his sleeve. "It's God's doin's, that's what it is."

"What does God have to do with this?" Nathan complained. "It's lousy luck, and it's not fair! I'm only twelve years old."

Mr. Thunder stood to his feet. "It's not bad luck. Don't you ever think this world is ruled by lucky breaks. Boy, providence is as different from luck as night is from day."

"I don't see any difference," Nathan whined.

"Did you ever watch a stamp mill?" Earl Thunder grabbed Nathan's shoulder and started leading him up the hill.

"Eh, no. What's that have to do with my lousy luck?" Nathan searched for a sign of the bear as they entered the big tin building. He squinted his eyes to adjust to the darkness inside and found himself staring at gigantic metal cylinders that looked like huge hammers without handles.

"What are those?" he questioned.

"The stamping machines," Mr. Thunder explained. "When this mine was running, some big steam engines powered the shafts to crush the rock into a fine powder. Then it's mixed with mercury, and the silver and gold is taken out. When this mill was going full force, you could hear these things thunder clear out to my place."

"What does that have to do with me?" Nathan asked.

"Well, some folks think the world is just one big stamp mill. Maybe you get crushed today, maybe tomorrow. Doesn't matter since there's nothing anyone can do about it. Folks like that end up bitter and mean."

"Yeah, that's what's happening to me. It isn't fair," Nathan added.

"That's where you're wrong." Mr. Thunder led Nathan back out into the sunlight of the Nevada hillside. "I say there's Someone in charge of things, and He knows what He's doing."

"You mean God?" Nathan mumbled.

"Exactly. Did your mother ever make you eat something you didn't want to?"

Nathan turned to look at Mr. Thunder. "Sure, like okra."

"And there was nothing you could do to get out of it, right?"

"Yeah," Nathan exclaimed. "Was your mom that way, too?"

Earl Thunder ignored the question and continued to explain. "So you felt helplessly caught up eating vegetables without a thing you could do about it?"

"Yeah, so what?" Nathan added.

"Well, son, why do you think your mother made you eat those things?"

"She said they were healthy, and they would keep me from getting sick," Nathan explained.

"So there you were—forced to do something you hadn't planned. But at least you had the confidence that it was for your own good."

"OK, OK." Nathan shrugged. "But what does this have to do with me now?"

"Maybe not finding your parents yet is for your own good. You have a choice to call it luck—or God's providence."

"Yeah, well . . . it's just the same no matter what I believe," Nathan continued. "Besides, how do you know for sure something has been providence?"

"You'll know. You'll know." Mr. Thunder put his hand on Nathan's shoulder. "Remember the difference. You don't have to be afraid of providence."

"I'm not afraid!" Nathan insisted. "And I'm going to find my parents!" He cleaned out his suitcase and made room for some food supplies. For a while no sounds were made other than the scraping of knives across the tin plates.

Lord, I just don't know anything anymore! I mean, I thought You wanted me to come out here.

"Well, Master Riggins, I'm hiking back to my claim. You're welcome to come stay with me a few days if you like," Earl Thunder offered.

"Thanks, but I'm not stopping until I find them." Nathan tossed his suitcase over his shoulder and shook Mr. Thunder's hand. "Thanks for the meal. I'm sure glad you were here."

"Providence, my boy," Earl Thunder said laughing, "just God's providence."

Nathan T. Riggins from Indiana left Willow Creek by the same road on which he had entered. The dog walked about twenty feet behind him. Big Belle Mountain overshadowed him on the south, but Nathan headed east to find the water supply that Earl Thunder had mentioned.

He was pleased that the new moccasins helped him keep a steady pace. From time to time he glanced back to spot the dog still trailing him. Although his energy was renewed by the big meal, Nathan was surprised at how long it took him to get to Trout Creek. He rested on its bank and filled his canteen and his stomach.

Nathan's plan was simple. He would hike around the base of Big Belle, camp near the crossroads, then walk on down to Galena, find a ride to Jersey, and rejoin his parents.

With any luck—or providence—or whatever, I can be with them by tomorrow night.

Instead of backtracking to the main Galena-Willow Creek trail, he followed the small creek downhill. After a considerable time of climbing over large rocks, Nathan found himself at the mouth of a canyon. At that point the creek just disappeared into the jagged rocks of the high desert floor.

Nathan yanked off his hat, wiped his sweaty forehead, and pushed his brown hair back off his ears. Then he squinted his eyes and stared at the horizon.

Where's Big Belle? Where's the crossroads? Where's Galena?

With the sun hovering straight above him, he could not even tell east from west.

A long series of rolling mountains stood in front of him as he left the small canyon. Nathan hiked to the top of the first ridge, expecting to spot Big Belle Mountain. Again he was disappointed.

Always looking back to make sure the dog followed, Nathan pushed on over one hill after another, searching for anything familiar. Finally, the hills died out, and only the flat high basin valley awaited them.

In the far distance across the long valley of sage, Nathan thought he spotted more mountains.

He turned and walked in the direction of the dog who now squatted down and waited for the hike to continue. "That's the Big Belle Mountain over there. It looks different from this angle, doesn't it?"

Then he took a swig of water from the canteen and pushed on out into the wilderness. The moccasins silenced his steps, and the only noise he heard was an occasional cry of a raven or hawk.

With no breeze, the sun blistered Nathan's skin, and the sweat from under his hat made streaks across his dusty face.

"This is really stupid!" Nathan complained to the dog, who always seemed to turn his head sideways and listen. "I don't want to be out here! Providence? Hardly!"

Halfway across the prairie, they came to a trail worn smooth by the constant traffic of animals. It was too sandy and dusty for Nathan to spot any particular footprints.

The dog crossed the trail and immediately trotted down it to the left.

"Hey, dog! That's the wrong direction. Come back here!" Nathan yelled.

The dog didn't slow down, so Nathan hurried to catch up. "Hey, come here! Really! I'm not going this way. If you don't turn around, I won't give you any food!"

Nathan rounded a bend in the trail, but the animal was nowhere in sight.

"Dog? Hey, dog! Where are you?" he called.

Suddenly, Nathan was alone again.

I am not lost. I will find Galena. I will go to Jersey. I will find my parents.

He hurried up the trail looking for the dog, yelling as he traveled, "Look, we are going the wrong direction! Come back here, right now!"

After about a mile of not seeing the dog, Nathan decided to turn back and go the other way. Spinning around, he stared at the dog walking along the trail behind him.

"So you circled back to push me along? Well, I hope you know where you're going."

Nathan reversed course again and plugged along, just ahead of the dog. His mind began to wander.

Apple pies! New clothes. A real bed with sheets. Mom will cry. Dad will get mad. I can help them find gold. We'll probably get rich and build one of those huge, three-story houses in Chicago. I'm going to buy me seven horses. A different one for every day of the week!

He stumbled out of his daydream at the shocking sight of an Indian riding a paint horse, coming right down the trail toward him. Nathan whipped around to escape, but behind him were three more mounted Indians, each carrying a rifle.

"Dog! I told you I didn't want to come down this trail!" he yelled out in panic.

The animal was nowhere in sight.

4

The minute Nathan broke from the trail towards the distant mountain, he knew it was the wrong thing to do.

They've got horses and guns!

He hadn't taken six steps before one of the Indians blocked his retreat and forced him at gunpoint back to the main path.

Almost as if listening to someone else, Nathan heard words tumble out of his mouth. "Listen! I'm Nathan T. Riggins from Indiana, and I'm supposed to be in Galena to find—"

The older Indian on the paint horse shouted something at the other men and then motioned at the moccasins on Nathan's feet. A very thin Indian with a long scar on his right arm dismounted and came over to Nathan.

"Not belong to you." He pointed to the beaded moccasins. "Give! Now!" He demanded with his hands.

Nathan spun from facing one Indian to another. "Look, these . . . I got these in a . . . Willow Creek, you know, at the store." He fought to hold back the tears.

"Belong to the son of Pie-a-ra-poo'-na." He reached

down and grabbed Nathan's right foot, causing him to sprawl backwards on the hot desert sand.

"OK, wait! You can have the moccasins." Nathan fumbled at the laces, pulling them off as quickly as he could.

Standing up barefoot, he noticed that another of the Indians was holding his leather suitcase.

Shifting from one foot to the other to keep them from burning, he protested, "Hey, that's my outfit! That's my knife! You can't have that!"

The thin Indian tossed the moccasins up to the older man and then remounted his own horse. "Go! Go!" He motioned Nathan on down the trail.

"My shoes! Give me my shoes! They're in the suitcase." Nathan could hear his voice breaking. "Please!"

"Go!" the Indian shouted, shoving the nozzle of his rifle between Nathan's shoulder blades.

Nathan's head spun. He couldn't figure out what to do. His stomach cramped, and he could hardly catch his breath. Yet he found himself stumbling along the dusty trail at the head of the column of four Indians. Every step shot fiery streaks of pain across his bare feet.

Lord, I don't want to die. Please, God. I just want Mom and Dad. I don't want to learn any more lessons! I can't take this . . . help me! . . . please, God, help me!

The afternoon was just a blur to Nathan. He was forced to jog at a fast trot. The Indians kept his canteen and his moccasins. Nathan knew his feet were blistered and bleeding, but they were so caked with dirt he could hardly tell. The sharp pains in his side turned to a dull, numbing throb. His mouth hung open, gasping for another breath.

Finally, they dropped into a draw where a small river twisted toward the distant mountains. Nathan sprinted to the water, shoving his feet in the cool mud and falling on his knees. Even though the water was only inches deep, he plunged his head under it, washing his face and drinking it in at the same time. Never in his life had water felt so good.

He came up gasping for air. Slinging his wet hair back and forth, he looked around to see where he was.

Along the far bank of the stream, several Indian children stared at him. Their black hair hung to their shoulders, and none of them wore shirts or shoes.

Behind the children Nathan noticed a half-dozen huge teepees, each wrapped with bleached buffalo hides. The Indians who had brought him in were now ahead of him, talking to a very old man who stood by the teepee in the middle of the others. Even from a distance Nathan could see his wrinkled, leathery face. The thin Indian with the scar splashed through the water and grabbed Nathan by the collar of his shirt, pulling him out of the river in the direction of the old man.

"You belong to Pie-a-ra-poo'-na," he gruffed.

The water dripped off Nathan's soaked clothing, and his feet, now clean, revealed the broken blisters from the burning trek across the desert floor.

"I've got to get back to Galena and find my parents," he appealed.

"You belong to Pie-a-ra-poo'-na!" the Indian insisted, turning to leave.

The old man stared at Nathan without smiling or speaking.

Suddenly a strong hand gripped his shoulder and pulled him toward the old man's teepee. Nathan jerked around to stare at a large Indian woman in a buckskin dress. Her face showed no sign of sympathy, but Nathan thought he caught a sign of kindness in her eyes. She pulled Nathan toward the teepee. "Come!" she barked. "Come, work!"

Inside the large smoky teepee, Nathan squinted to focus on the shadowy figures moving around the coals of the circle fire in the center. Even before he could tell how many women and children occupied the teepee, the big woman shoved him and a young girl out the entryway.

"You bring back firewood—or else!" she ordered.

Nathan walked behind the girl, who looked several years younger. His mind was starting to clear.

As soon as we're out of their sight, I'll push the girl down and run for it. Maybe I can hide in a cave or something. I'll just make a run all the way back to Galena!

Not more than one hundred steps beyond the last teepee, the girl turned around and startled Nathan with a question.

"My name's Eetahla. What is your name?"

"What? You speak English?" Nathan choked.

"Yes. I was taught by a missionary lady. But that was before I came to live with the Newe."

"The Newe?"

She pointed toward the teepees.

"Newe? I've never heard of that tribe," Nathan offered.

The young girl began to break off dead pieces of sagebrush and started piling them on the dirt. "Newe, you know, the Shoshone."

"And . . . you're not one of them?" Nathan started helping Eetahla pile up the wood.

"No!" she insisted. "I do not even look like them!"

Nathan didn't mention that he thought she looked exactly like the others.

"I am Ne-mee-poo, Nez Perce. My people live far to the north. You did not tell me your name."

She worked quickly, gathering wood even as she talked.

"I'm Nathan T. Riggins from Indiana," he announced.

"You are Indian? You lie. You are too white. Except for your feet. They are red," she giggled.

"No, from Indiana. It's a state. You know, like Ohio, Nevada, or California," Nathan explained.

"And I say you are not Indian," she repeated.

Nathan changed the subject. "If these are not your people, why are you here?"

"My family became sick and died while we were down on the Snake River two years ago. Pie-a-ra-poo'-na found me alive, and he lets me eat at his fire," she explained.

"Why don't you run away?" Nathan suggested.

"And go where? I do not know this land. Besides they have warriors watching us even now."

Nathan quickly scanned the horizon. "Where? Where are they? I don't see anybody."

"It is as I say," Eetahla repeated.

"Well, I'm going to run away," Nathan insisted.

"It is not wise." She shrugged. Then, looking down at the ground where Nathan stood, she continued the conversation, "Do your feet hurt?"

"Like walking on a carpet of sewing needles," he groaned. "They would probably hurt more, but I'm too scared to think about them."

"When we get back to the teepee, I'll find you some poohi-natesua," Eetahla offered.

"What's that?"

She climbed a few steps up the side of a dirt ridge and grabbed at some dead tree roots. "It's a kind of medicine. Did you know that my name, Eetahla, means . . . Aieee! No! No!"

Chills ran down Nathan's back as she let out an ear-piercing scream. Unable to move his feet, he looked up to see a small rattlesnake about twelve inches long hanging from Eetahla's arm.

Continuing to scream, she flung her arm wildly, and the baby snake flew off toward Nathan. It landed at his feet, but he just stood and stared.

"Kill it! Kill it!" Eetahla screamed.

Nathan watched hypnotically as the snake coiled itself to strike at his swollen feet.

In a shadowy flash and a snap of the teeth, the gray

and white dog suddenly dashed from a nearby sagebrush. He pounced on the snake, grabbing it in his mouth right behind its head. With a violent shake, the dog sent snake parts scattering across the desert floor.

"Is that your dog?" Eetahla cried.

"Eh, yeah, I guess . . . I mean we were hiking together." Nathan stared at the fang marks on her arm.

"Give me your belt, quick," she screamed. "Then go get Gwee-ya."

Nathan stripped off his belt and helped Eetahla wrap it around her arm several inches above the bite.

"Gwee-ya . . . Pie-a-ra-poo'-na's wife. Tell her to hurry. I need the hakinop. Hurry!"

Suddenly Eetahla turned a sickly yellow and then collapsed in the sand.

"Eetahla!" Nathan panicked. "Eetahla!"

Without thinking, he reached down and picked her up and started running back to camp. His arms ached, and his feet blazed, but he hardly noticed.

She's dead . . . No! No! She's dead!

Nathan hadn't noticed that he was screaming as he entered camp. Suddenly, he realized everyone was watching him. Placing Eetahla by the entrance to the teepee, he yelled for Gwee-ya, who took one look at the unconscious girl and dashed back inside. Running out of the teepee carrying a knife and a bag of roots, Gwee-ya knelt by Eetahla.

Nathan watched as the knife sliced into Eetahla's arm. He felt his head get very light . . . Gwee-ya was talking to him, but she sounded miles away. Then she grabbed a wild root out of the bag and quickly mashed it between two rocks.

Nathan thought he saw Gwee-ya smear the pulp on Eetahla's arm and tie it there with a strap of deerhide. Then, all at once, he saw nothing.

■

Voices from the other side of the buffalo hide nudged at Nathan's mind, and he quickly sat straight up. Instead of lying out in front of the teepee, he was inside by the fire. Instead of daylight, it was now dark. Instead of staring at Eetahla, she was now staring at him.

"What happened?" Nathan whispered, as he glanced at the others asleep around the fire pit.

"You went to sleep," Eetahla replied as she propped herself up on one elbow.

"Went to sleep? But you were dead . . . I mean, the snake and—"

"Dead?" Eetahla laid her head back on the ground. "I do not feel very good, but I do not feel so bad as to be dead. You and your dog saved me."

"Me? I didn't do anything but freeze up and faint." Nathan also lay down and continued to whisper.

"That's not what Pie-a-ra-poo'-na says. He said—"

Nathan rolled over and looked at Eetahla. "Who is he?"

"He happens to be the chief of the To-na-wits'-o-wa Shoshone. He is a very important man," Eetahla

49

instructed. "Anyway, he said it takes a strong warrior to run to camp carrying me, especially with weak feet."

Nathan suddenly remembered his aching feet.

"Well, I didn't know what to do with the snake," he sighed.

"Your dog is very good at killing snakes." Eetahla tried to smile.

"Did I really faint when she cut your arm?" Nathan questioned.

"I was asleep, too," Eetahla offered, "but when I woke up, Gwee-ya told me all about what you did. She said that I was lucky to have a strong warrior with me, or I could have died."

"Maybe it was providence that I was here," Nathan suggested.

Eetahla lifted her coal black eyebrows. "Providence?"

"It's nothing." Nathan lay still and listened to the voices outside the teepee.

"Eetahla?"

"Yes?"

"Are they talking about me?" Nathan asked.

"Yes."

Nathan propped himself up on one elbow and whispered, "What are they saying?"

"Something about you and the dog. I don't know. I am very tired. Good night." Then she rolled over and lay silent.

Nathan looked up at the crest of the teepee. He

could see stars in the sky through the small smoke opening in the center.

I can't believe this. Last night I was alone on Big Belle Mountain—and now . . . Lord, it's me, Nathan T. Riggins from Indiana. Things aren't going so good. I'm really worried. I think it would be a very good time for me to find Mom and Dad. And, eh, well, I'm glad Eetahla didn't die. Thank You.

When Nathan woke up, Gwee-ya was cooking on the fire in the middle of the teepee, but no one else was inside. He sat up and rubbed his eyes, looking at the early morning light breaking on the camp outside the teepee.

"Where is Eetahla?" he asked.

"Getting wood." Gwee-ya nodded.

"Is she . . . still sick?" He stuck out his feet and inspected their cuts and blisters.

"Eetahla is strong girl. She will get well. And you are strong boy. You talk to Pie-a-ra-poo'-na now."

"Me? He wants to talk to me? I mean, will he speak to me in English?" Nathan stammered.

"No. Eetahla will talk for you. Go."

Nathan carefully placed each foot as he stepped out into the morning air. The dew on the grass cooled his still stinging feet.

Sitting at a campfire was the old chief and several other men. Eetahla brought an armful of firewood to the opening of Gwee-ya's teepee and then walked alongside Nathan.

"Am I supposed to talk to him?" Nathan asked her.

"Yes," she instructed. "Sit straight across the fire from Pie-a-ra-poo'-na."

Nathan limped over to the fire and sat down. He noticed that none of the men smiled or nodded. In fact, he could see no expression in their tanned and wrinkled faces. Eetahla stood behind him.

Suddenly Pie-a-ra-poo'-na pointed at him and spoke.

Eetahla interpreted, "He asks, 'Does that dog belong to you?'"

Nathan looked beyond the teepees to see the gray and white dog lying in a crouch, with eyes focused on the group at the campfire.

"Well, sort of, I mean, the dog sort of—"

"Is he your dog?" Eetahla insisted.

Nathan took a deep breath and muttered, "I do not own the dog, but we are . . . friends, traveling together."

She repeated the words to the white-haired chief. Nathan thought he noticed the beginning of a smile on his face. Then Pie-a-ra-poo'-na spoke again.

"He wants to know the name of the dog," Eetahla said.

"Eh, well, tell the chief that the dog has not yet told me his name," Nathan stammered.

When Eetahla translated Nathan's words, the old chief grinned from ear to ear, and the other men at the campfire began to laugh.

Nathan felt panic coming on. "Did I say something wrong?" he asked Eetahla.

"Oh, no," she beamed. "You have answered very well."

For the next several minutes Pie-a-ra-poo'-na lectured the whole group, and Eetahla did not interrupt to translate. Finally the chief was finished. Then he picked up a bundle of clothing and passed it around the fire circle to Nathan.

"What did he say? What is this?" Nathan quizzed.

"He said you did well to carry me into camp last night. But these clothes are because of Tona-we-a."

"Tona-we-a?"

"The dog's name is Tona-we-a," Eetahla explained. "You see, that dog used to belong to Pie-a-ra=poo'-na's grandson. But his grandson died last winter, and the dog ran away from camp. He said his grandson was a very brave warrior and that Tona-we-a would only become friends with you if you, too, were a brave warrior. So he returns your moccasins and gives you this deerskin shirt. They used to belong to his grandson."

"You mean they like me because of that dog?" Nathan asked.

Eetahla smiled, "Yes, they said Tona-we-a has good judgment."

"Can I leave now? I mean, can I go find my parents?" Nathan's voice showed his excitement.

She asked the chief and then repeated his answer. "Yes, you may leave any time you wish, but he says you should stay until after we eat," she advised. "It is a long way to town."

Nathan carried his new clothing as he and Eetahla walked back to Gwee-ya's teepee.

"Eetahla," Nathan asked, "what does Tona-we-a mean?"

She flipped her braided black hair behind her shoulders and shrugged. "I think it means 'no-smile dog.'"

5

Nathan had pulled on his moccasins and was exchanging his dirty shirt for the soft deerskin pullover shirt when he heard shouts and gun-shots from just beyond the camp.

Racing out of the teepee, he felt relief to discover a celebration going on as an old trader, with a wagon full of goods, pulled into the small Shoshone settlement.

Eetahla ran up to him shouting, "It's Dawson! Come on, it's Dawson!"

Her enthusiasm excited Nathan. "Who's Dawson?" He huffed as he tried to keep up.

"He has all sorts of very pretty cloth, and pans, and knives," Eetahla shouted, "and candy! Sometimes he even has candy!"

By the time they reached the wagon, Mr. Dawson was standing at the back of the rig, displaying a cast-iron Dutch oven to Gwee-ya and several other Shoshone women. At first glance, Nathan figured him to be over six feet tall, but then he noticed that the gray-bearded trader was standing on a wooden box. He chattered in Shoshone as fluently as Eetahla and seemed to have the whole tribe spellbound with his pitch. The floppy, black wide-brimmed hat on his head shaded his face, but even so, Mr. Dawson looked as dark-skinned as the Indians.

Nathan was staring at a bright blue and red blanket when he realized that the man was talking to him.

"I say, son—son? What are you doing with the To-na-wits'-o-wa? You can talk, can't ya?"

"What? Oh, y-yes," Nathan stuttered. "I'm Nathan T. Riggins from Indiana."

"Well, I'm Marcus Dawson, from Ragtown to Ft. McDermitt, from Austin to Elko and most every point in between. I sell dry goods and housewares," the old man announced. "But you still didn't say what you're doing here."

"I'm trying to find my parents who were supposed to be in Willow Creek, but they aren't, so I'm going to Galena to catch a stage to Jersey," Nathan blurted out.

"Son, I don't think I'm gettin' through to you." Mr. Dawson just shook his head. "Why are you here in this Shoshone camp?"

"I got lost," Nathan admitted.

"Am I going to have to trade a blanket to get you away from these pals of yours?" Dawson asked.

"No, I'm free to walk away. But I thought I'd wait for breakfast and then hike back to Galena."

"Well, it's a good twenty miles to Galena. You'd better hitch a ride with me," Mr. Dawson suggested. "Do you know horses?"

"Yes, sir," Nathan stammered. "I worked with my grandfather's team back in—"

"Indiana," Dawson interrupted, "yeah, I got that

much. Well, you unhitch that team and lead them over to the river. After they've watered, take them to that far bank and stake them out until I'm done here. Then I'll give you a lift into Galena."

"Yes sir!" Nathan raced to the front of the wagon and began to unhitch the team.

Suddenly, life seemed to be improving.

Maybe it's that I'm not afraid of the Indians now. Maybe it's Mr. Dawson showing up to give me a ride. Maybe it's the bright blue sky, the clean air, and the fresh, flowing stream. Maybe it's the feel of moccasins on sore feet. Maybe it's having done something right by helping Eetahla. Maybe it's . . . Nathan glanced downstream to see the dog crouched in the weeds, watching him. *Maybe it's Tona-we-a. Anyway, thanks, Lord.*

Mr. Dawson's horses were not nearly as big as the ones Nathan's grandfather had used on the farm in Indiana. But their calm nature and easy stride reminded Nathan of the past. He led them to a small patch of grass along the river and sat down between them. Nathan stretched his arms out and yawned. He laid back and closed his eyes, but immediately felt uneasy. Opening his eyes he saw two long black braids and Eetahla's smiling face above him.

He jumped to his feet. "What are you doing?" he demanded.

Eetahla laughed and took a stick of candy out of her mouth. "Do you want some?" she offered.

"No! I mean, yes." Nathan fumbled for words. "I'll go ask Dawson for a piece for myself."

"Are you going with him?" she asked.

"Yes. He's going to give me a ride to Galena."

She smoothed back her bangs to reveal a dirty face. "Why are you going?"

"To find my father and my mother," Nathan explained once more. "How about you, Eetahla? Are you going to search for your family?"

"Why should I do that? I know where they are. They are dead." She jammed the stick candy back into her mouth.

"So you will stay with Pie-a-ra-poo'-na?" Nathan asked.

"Yes. At least until a brave warrior carries me off." Eetahla waded out into the stream and wiggled her toes in the mud. Then she washed her sticky hands. Nathan noticed she didn't bother washing her face.

"What do you mean, carry you off?" he quizzed.

"When I become his wife," she smiled, showing a full mouth of gleaming teeth. "I want to be like Gwee-ya."

"Oh, yeah . . . well," Nathan said, "I think it's time to get the team back to Mr. Dawson."

"White boy," Eetahla squinted her eyes and dropped her head to one side as she asked, "if you and I were more years, and you were a brave warrior, would you carry me off?"

Nathan felt his face flush. *Eetahla is starting to sound just like Melissa!* "Eh, sure. I mean, I think I would, you know, if we were older."

"I thought so," she giggled. Suddenly, without

effort, Eetahla jumped up, grabbed the black mane on the bay mare and pulled herself up on top of the horse.

"How did you do that?" Nathan gasped as he looked up at the height of the horse.

"Do what?" she asked.

"Nothing," Nathan sighed. He wasn't about to try the same feat and be embarrassed by a girl. He led the two horses, with Eetahla mounted on one of them, back to Mr. Dawson's wagon.

While Nathan went with Eetahla and Gwee-ya to eat some breakfast, Mr. Dawson hooked up his team and reloaded the wagon. Nathan figured the sun was at about 10:00 A.M. when the old trader pulled around to Pie-a-ra-poo'-na's teepee. Grabbing his small leather suitcase that had been returned to him, Nathan climbed up on the wagon.

He whistled and called out, "Hey, dog! Come on!" The gray and white dog skirted the camp and circled out in front of the wagon, leading the way. Nathan turned back and waved at his friends.

Pie-a-ra-poo'-na and several men sat around the outdoor fire ring, playing some kind of game by hiding sticks in the palms of their hands. They ignored the departing wagon. Gwee-ya stood by the teepee entrance with a new bright purple and scarlet piece of cloth tied around her neck. She waved at Nathan.

He spotted Eetahla far back in the teepee. She was holding the candy stick in her left hand. She stared, blank-faced, straight at Nathan. She didn't wave.

"You're a lucky lad you found them in good spirits," Mr. Dawson growled.

"You mean . . . the Indians?" Nathan squirmed on the wagon seat, trying to find a comfortable position.

"What I mean is, two months ago, Pie-a-ra-poo'-na was down in the Ruby Mountains fightin' Utes and miners."

"A fight?" Nathan asked, "You mean, with bows and arrows?"

"Bows, arrows, knives, rocks, spears, pistols, and Winchester repeating rifles," Mr. Dawson reported.

"Who won?" Nathan demanded.

"The army. When the troops showed up, the fightin' pretty well stopped."

Nathan and Marcus Dawson talked off and on for the next two hours. When the sun was straight overhead, they stopped in the middle of the sagebrush and ate a cold dinner of beans, bread, and canned tomatoes.

"Can I feed something to my dog?" Nathan asked.

"That dog ought to feed us," Mr. Dawson laughed. "Look at him!"

Nathan spotted the dog about thirty feet on up the trail. "What's he got in his mouth?"

"A jackrabbit," Mr. Dawson said.

"What kind of rabbit?" Nathan pulled his hat down to shade his eyes, trying to get a better look at the dog and its lunch.

Marcus rubbed his chin whiskers and answered, "A long-eared hare. They call them jackrabbits out here."

When they started back up the trail, once again the

dog took the lead. Most of the time he trotted twenty feet ahead of the wagon. Sometimes he would disappear for quite a while. Then suddenly he was back out front.

An hour or more after they ate, Nathan glanced across the floor of the valley and noticed a plume of dust swirling several miles ahead of the them. "Is that more Indians up there?" he pointed.

"Could be. Or it could be just a dust devil. Or some prospectors. Or some wild horses. Or some wild men." Nathan noticed that Mr. Dawson kept his eyes on the dust plume, but he reached behind the wagon seat and lifted out a double-barreled shotgun. "There are worse problems than Indians," he announced.

Nathan sat silent. His mind raced back to the copy of *Frank Leslie's Illustrated Newspaper* that he had read on the train as it left Omaha. It was a story entitled "The Last Stage to Indian Wells."

Tahoe Mason had been at the reins when he was confronted by the notorious Milborn brothers. During the shootout, Ott Milborn took a shotgun blast in the leg, which left him crippled the rest of his life. But Tahoe received only a slight wound in the arm and was able to protect Miss Larissa.

Of course, that's what happened in the story. Now Nathan wondered if another Frank Leslie adventure was about to take place before his eyes. But when he looked up, the column of dust had vanished.

"Hey, look at that. It's gone! Probably was just a whirlwind," Nathan proclaimed.

Marcus Dawson didn't respond to Nathan, but

instead he cracked the shotgun and inspected the chambers to make sure two shells were in place.

"Well, if someone was hiding out, it would be right at the Reese River crossing," Mr. Dawson announced. "If we make it through the water, we'll be safe."

He pulled the wagon up to the top of the bluff overlooking the crossing and stopped. After surveying the scrubby cottonwood trees along the river, Mr. Dawson turned to Nathan. "All right, son, let's see what we got. Could be I got jumpy for nothin'."

The dog shot across the river and disappeared behind the far embankment with a yelp.

"He must have caught another rabbit," Nathan suggested.

The team of horses trotted right up to the shallow water's edge. Then they high-stepped into the muddy stream. Nathan could not spot any sign of trouble and began to scold himself for letting his imagination run away with him. Just then something back in the scrubby trees caught his attention when they were halfway across the water.

"Look! There's a down horse!" Nathan shouted above the sound of splashing. "And it's still saddled!"

"They rode it to death or shot it," Mr. Dawson offered.

"Aren't we going to stop?" Nathan pressed.

"Well, if there is a man on foot, I suppose we ought to check it out." Mr. Dawson pulled the team out the far side of the stream. They rolled up to the horse, and Mr.

Dawson got up to check the surrounding trees and brush. He handed the reins to Nathan.

"Son, if something ain't square here, you just slap those horses and get yourself on down the road. You got that?"

Nathan looked around and nodded his head as Mr. Dawson climbed off the wagon and walked toward the horse.

"Well, he's still breathin'," Mr. Dawson called out. He reached down and grabbed the loose reins, trying to raise the horse's head and get the animal on its feet. The horse didn't budge at all. Finally, Dawson laid down his shotgun and reached around the neck of the animal, trying to bring it up.

At that moment, Nathan heard a shrill whistle from behind the wagon. Suddenly the horse bolted to its feet, knocking Marcus Dawson to the ground. Nathan whipped around towards the sound and stared right into the masked face of a man in a big black hat pointing a pistol at Mr. Dawson.

He motioned with his head toward Nathan. "Climb off the wagon and get over by your old man!" he ordered.

Nathan tumbled off the wagon and hurried over to Mr. Dawson.

Keeping his gun pointed directly at the two of them, the man rummaged through the wagonload of goods with the other hand.

"Where's your guns and whiskey?" he demanded.

"Ain't got none," Mr. Dawson replied.

"You were just down at that Indian camp, weren't you?"

Mr. Dawson noted how far away the shotgun was and then looked back at the man. "Yep, I was down there. But I don't sell guns or liquor to any man, especially Indians."

"That's a lie! No trader in Nevada would go without guns and whiskey," the outlaw insisted.

"It's the truth," Nathan blurted out. "I was there in the camp, and they didn't buy any of that stuff."

"Mister, if you find any guns and liquor, then you can keep it," Dawson promised.

"Listen, old man, I can have everything in this whole wagon!" he argued. "And quit eyeing that shotgun. I go plumb crazy when someone tries to shoot me."

The man pulled a rope off the side of the wagon and tied Mr. Dawson to the spokes of the front left wheel. Then he tied Nathan to the front right wheel.

For the next several minutes the bandit ransacked the entire wagon, tossing most of the goods out into the dust. In order to save time, he jammed his pistol back into his pants, and used two hands for digging through the wagonload of goods.

"A gold trigger!" Nathan mumbled.

"What did you say?" the man growled.

"The boy's just scared," Mr. Dawson interrupted. "You got no reason to tie him up."

"I shot a man when I was his age. I think I'll leave the ropes on."

The gunman took mainly food items, some knives,

a couple pistols, and ammunition from all the goods in the wagon.

"Where's my dog?" Nathan called out.

"That mutt belongs to you? I should have known you were a half-breed, what with the moccasins and jacket."

"Did you shoot him?" Nathan was almost in tears.

"Waste a good bullet on a dog? I just popped him with a log. He'll wake up in a day or so, if I didn't split his skull."

Just at that moment, without even a growl, the dog came leaping over the wagon and tore into the outlaw's leg. The masked bandit let out a yell and kicked the dog across the clearing.

Nathan stared in horror as the man grabbed up the shotgun and fired it at the dog. But before Nathan could open his mouth, the team of horses, frightened by the dual shotgun blasts, bolted up the far embankment.

Tied to the wheel, the boy took one crashing spin around the wheel and then passed out.

6

*T*he very first thing Nathan noticed was the sand in his mouth.

Then he realized that it was dark. And finally, though he was still in a daze, the throbbing of battered and bruised legs demanded his attention.

He spat out the sand and rolled over on his back. He didn't even try to stand. The diamond-sprinkled night sky seemed unconcerned with his condition.

Struggling to establish a breathing pattern, Nathan propped himself up on one elbow and looked around. The tiny sliver of a moon offered little light to see his surroundings.

The wagon! Shotgun blast! The dog? He killed my dog!

"Mr. Dawson . . . Mr. Dawson!" Nathan called out.

There was no answer.

No sound.

No movement.

Nothing.

Nathan reached around trying to discover what was near him. All he felt was the sandy dirt of the high desert floor. He considered standing, but his legs still ached. He began to examine his body. The deerskin shirt seemed to be dusty, but it was still holding together. There was a rip clear to the knee on the right leg of his trousers, and his right foot was bare.

He tried to rub his legs, but they felt like a hundred bruises. His hat was missing, and there was a lot of dirt in his hair. Nathan took a deep breath and held his knees to his chest.

"I've just got to wait it out until daylight," he mumbled, still tasting dirt and sand.

■

When Nathan awoke, he was still sitting up holding his knees. Daylight had began to break over a distant ridge of eastern mountains. Although the sun was not yet in sight, Nathan could see fairly well in the early light. He jumped to his feet, took a step, and immediately fell to the ground.

"Tona-we-a!" The dog's name popped out of Nathan's mouth before he could even think. It was the first time he had called the dog by name. Sitting not more than twenty feet away was the gray and white dog.

"Come here, boy!" Nathan called. "Come on! Are you all right?"

The dog slinked towards Nathan, stopped about ten feet away, and once again settled into a defensive crouch.

"Come on, come on!" Nathan called.

The dog did not move.

"Well, at least I've got you," Nathan sighed and

again stood to his feet. This time he stayed in one place until his head cleared, and then he began to walk slowly, slightly limping on his bare right foot.

The dog moved in about five feet behind Nathan and followed him. Just behind a sagebrush Nathan discovered part of Mr. Dawson's wagon. In fact the only things missing were the left front wheel, the tongue, and the two horses. The back end of the trailer was broken, and there were no supplies left in the wagon. The spokes were broken out of the front wheel, and ropes lay scattered about on the ground.

Nathan shuddered as he followed the skid marks of the broken wagon. "We came right over that rim and busted up down here." He pointed to the wagon carcass. "I guess I tumbled off the wheel when it broke up."

Limping less, but still hurting, Nathan and the dog hiked up the twelve-foot slope and started to trace the wagon tracks backwards.

"Riggins! Is that you over there?"

"Mr. Dawson? Mr. Dawson, where are you?" Nathan called out.

"Under this blasted wheel in the sage. Get me out of here!"

Heading toward the voice, Nathan found Marcus Dawson still tied to the fourth wheel and face down in a huge sagebrush.

"Are you all right?" he called as he reached the wheel.

"All right? All right? I'd rather be dead than feel this

bad," Dawson moaned. "Reach in my pocket and get my knife to cut off these ropes."

Nathan cut the ropes and pried the wheel to one side, allowing Mr. Dawson to slide out onto the desert floor. The older man yelped with pain and then just lay there and looked at his tangled legs.

Finally he asked, "How did you get free?"

"I guess my wheel busted its spokes, and I crashed off that rim down there. I woke up last night and then passed out again." Nathan just stared at Mr. Dawson. "What's wrong with your legs?"

"They're broke, that's what! I see your dog survived. That's grand."

Nathan looked back at the dog. "Yes, I thought for sure he'd be dead."

"Well, that shotgun shoots two feet high. I've been meaning to fix those sights. Don't guess I will now," Mr. Dawson groaned. "Son, did you say the wagon is down off that rim?"

"Yes sir," Nathan replied, "but it's all busted up."

"And the horses? Did you see the horses?" he quizzed.

Nathan stared at Mr. Dawson's twisted legs. "Uh, no, I didn't see the horses."

"Well, Nathan T. Riggins of Indiana, it's about time you learned a little about frontier doctoring. I want you to go down there and tear four pieces of timber from the wagon bed or sides. I need them about two feet long. I've got to splint these legs," Mr. Dawson stated.

Nathan hurried down off the rim with Tona-we-a

once again following him. It was not hard to find several broken wagon boards. Returning to Mr. Dawson, Nathan found the old trader sitting up, staring at his legs.

"Now, son, I'm going to have to ask you to do a man's job. Wouldn't ask no lad to do this, but there just ain't no other way. Now you listen up 'cause most of the work will be up to you." Dawson took a deep breath. "We've got to straighten those legs and splint them."

"Straighten them?" Nathan gasped, "Won't that hurt?"

"I reckon it will feel like a train running over me, but it's got to be done. Now listen careful. I need you to sit on that right leg and push down on it until it flattens out. Then put a splint on both sides of it and tie it with . . . eh, tie it with the rawhide ties in your leggins."

Nathan still stared at the man's twisted legs.

"Then do the same thing on the left leg."

"But," Nathan stammered, "I lost my other moccasin. I mean, I've only got one lacing."

"Well," Mr. Dawson grouched, "I don't think that dog of yours needs to wear the other one!"

"What?" Nathan spun around and spotted the dog carrying the other moccasin in his mouth. "You found my moccasin!"

The dog walked up to within five feet of Nathan, dropped the beaded moccasin, and then backed off.

Nathan quickly pulled it on his sore right foot and stripped the lacing out of each one. "Now what?" he asked.

"You're going to push down on that right leg,"

Dawson said. "Now listen up, son. When you push on that leg, I am going to scream to high heaven. I'll yell, cry, call you names, and threaten to kill you, but you do it anyway. And as soon as you get the first one tight, straighten the other one."

"Eh, couldn't we wait until we find a doctor?" Nathan suggested.

"Son, I'll die out here in the wilderness if you don't set those legs," Mr. Dawson commanded.

"Lord, help us," Nathan mumbled.

"He will, boy." Mr. Dawson nodded. "He will."

Nathan went around and leaned on the distorted right leg.

"Do it quick, boy, do it quick," Mr. Dawson barked, with sweat rolling down his face.

Pushing all other thoughts from his mind, Nathan lunged onto the leg. It snapped, and Dawson let out an ear-piercing scream. Spinning around to look the old man in the eyes, he saw that Dawson had passed out. With the man silent, Nathan hurried to strap on the splints and tie them tight. Then he did the same thing, with the same sickening snap, on the left leg. When he finished, he sat looking at Mr. Dawson, waiting for him to come to.

Tona-we-a suddenly darted off into the desert sage, and Nathan pursued the dog.

Lord, it's me again. This would be a very good time for You to show me what to do next. I don't know how to get to Galena, and I don't know how to get Mr. Dawson there. I don't even know if Mr. Dawson is still alive.

71

Tona-we-a's constant barking interrupted his conversation.

He looked up to see the dog circling the two horses.

"The team! You found Mr. Dawson's horses!" Nathan shouted.

The horses were still hitched together, but all they pulled was the broken tongue of the trader's wagon. Nathan led the team back toward Mr. Dawson. When he reached the clearing, the old trader was still unconscious.

Somehow, I've got to get Mr. Dawson on one of those horses.

The sun was straight overhead, and still Mr. Dawson lay motionless. Finally Nathan hiked back to the wagon and began to pull off the two sideboards. Each one was about a foot wide and ten feet long. Working steadily, he dragged the boards back to Mr. Dawson and laid them side by side, like a stretcher, next to the old man. With considerable pushing and shoving, he rolled Mr. Dawson over onto the wagon slats. Bringing the team straight behind the downed trader, Nathan carefully eased the team forward until they straddled Mr. Dawson. Crawling in between the horses, he struggled to lift the head end of the makeshift stretcher and lash it to the wagon tongue with some broken harness leather.

Nathan walked backwards, leading the team and watching to see what would happen to the unconscious man. He seemed to ride along on the dragging stretcher without any problem other than gathering dust from the horses' hoofs.

Surveying the mountain range to the west, Nathan

thought he could make out the silhouette of Big Belle Mountain.

"If that's Big Belle," Nathan told Tona-we-a, "then Galena is straight ahead on this side!" With the dog leading the way, Nathan led the team towards the west. After about an hour, he remembered how Eetahla so easily pulled herself to the top of this same horse. Nathan reached up and grabbed the horse's mane with his left hand, threw his right arm up on the withers, and jumped up towards the horse's back.

Hitting the horse squarely on the side, Nathan cracked to the ground with a small handful of black horsehair. Finally, he walked between the two horses, put one foot on the stretcher behind Mr. Dawson's head, and jumped to the back of the left horse. Clutching with all his strength, he pulled his left leg over and straddled the horse. Glancing down at Marcus Dawson, Nathan kicked the horse and the team began to move.

■

At first it was just a white reflection on the horizon. Then as they moved closer step by slow step, the shimmer of tent tops began to take shape.

"It's Galena! We made it, Tona, we made it!" Nathan shouted.

The dog made no reply, but as usual it faded into the sage as Nathan and the horses entered town.

In most eastern towns, the sight of a tattered boy wearing an Indian shirt and moccasins, riding a team of horses, dragging a wagon slat with an unconscious man aboard would certainly have captured the attention of nearly everyone.

In Galena, Nevada, no one even bothered to look up.

"Hey, mister," Nathan yelled at a man unhitching his horse, "where's the doctor's office?"

"Doctor? Have we got a doc?" the man yelled back.

"My friend is hurt bad," Nathan called out.

The man saddled up and spun his horse toward the building he had just exited. Then he called in through the open doorway, "Hey, Kerby! Is there a doctor in this town?"

A short man with a full black beard stepped out onto the wooden sidewalk. "Sure, we got a doc. I just saw Stryker down at the Wild Horse Cafe."

"Stryker's a doctor?" the man questioned.

"During the war, he was," Kerby explained.

"Well, you heard him, son. Check down at the Wild Horse. Clear on the other side of town."

Nathan rode on down the main street and came upon three men digging a deep hole right in the middle of the street. He stopped and peeked over the mound of dirt to see what the men were doing.

Unable to see anything, he started up the team again, only to see the barefoot girl he had spoken to several days before.

"Did you find your ma and your daddy?" she asked him. Then, before he could answer, she continued, "Where'd you get them Indian clothes? Where's your old shoes? I'll take your old shoes if you don't want them. Who's that man? Is he dead?"

Nathan kept the team moving. "No, I didn't find my parents; Indians gave me this jacket. No, you can't have my old shoes because I lost them, and, no, the man's not dead." For the first time Nathan thought about how ragged he must look.

Jumping off the horse, he walked past a line of men waiting to eat at the Wild Horse Cafe.

"Is there a Mr. Stryker in here?" he called out.

He glanced through the crowded room and called out again, "Mr., I mean, Dr. Stryker?"

Suddenly a tall, thin man with red hair spun around on his bench.

"Are you Dr. Stryker?" Nathan asked.

"Yep, but most folks just call me Stryker," the man replied.

"Well, Mr. Dawson, a trader, got hurt real bad. I think both legs are broken. I need you to come take a look at him."

The doctor scraped a final bite from his plate and called out to another man, "Come on, Wacey, I might need some help."

As Nathan turned to scurry to the front of the tent-covered building, he looked across the room and saw the man who had been on the stage from Battle Mountain Station three days before just entering the cafe.

It's him! It's the man with the gold trigger!

Nathan kept out of the man's sight as he slipped out. Doctor Stryker put his ear to Mr. Dawson's chest and then quickly unlashed the sideboard stretcher. "Wacey, it's Marcus Dawson under all that dust. Grab that end and let's take him over to the hotel. He's still alive. Son, what happened? Did he get his legs run over by a wagon?"

"Sort of. Listen, I need to talk to the sheriff," Nathan pressed.

"Well, we do have a town marshall." Stryker nodded.

"Where can I find him?" Nathan urged.

"That's easy. Down at the bottom of that hole in the street."

Nathan missed his hat. He shaded the bright sun with his hand. "What are they doing down there—digging a well?"

"Well? They're after gold, son, just like everyone else," Stryker laughed.

"Gold? In the middle of the street?" Nathan asked.

"Yeah, and if they find any, we'll probably tear down the whole town looking for more."

"Look, I'll be back in a minute. I've got to go find the marshall." Nathan's legs ached as he ran down the street toward the big hole.

7

Nathan T. Riggins, formerly of Indiana, would have been completely shocked at the way he looked, if he had had time to gaze in a mirror.

The slightly frumpy eastern-boy look had disappeared. His face was a tough reddish bronze with a generous layer of dirt. The deerskin shirt and moccasins were well worn from the terrifying ride while he was strapped to the wagon wheel. His trousers were dirty and torn. His hands were blistered. His hair had not been combed for two days. He looked as if he had spent his last ten years in the wilds.

Actually, Nathan looked like every other kid in Nevada.

Climbing up on the mound of loose dirt, he peered down into the pit in the center of the street. Two men were pulling up buckets of dirt tied to ropes, while the third man was at the bottom of a twenty-foot hole, filling the buckets as fast as he could.

"Son, you better get down from there. A fella could fall and get hurt."

Nathan looked up to see one of the men with a rope and bucket motioning to him.

"I need to talk to the marshall!" Nathan blurted out.

"He's in the hole," the man pointed. "Kholey! There's a kid here to see you. Marshall business, he says."

"I'm busy now, son. Check with me at suppertime." Marshall Kholey kept shoveling.

"Marshall, sir, a man, Mr. Marcus Dawson . . . he's a trader. Well, he got robbed, and now he's hurt pretty bad, and I know who did it. The man's eating dinner over at the Wild Horse Cafe, and I think you better come quick!" Nathan shouted without catching his breath.

Marshall Kholey huffed up the homemade ladder and out of the hole. Turning to one of the other men, he barked orders, "Liddon, you go down and spell me. I don't think we're more than a foot from bedrock. I need to do some marshallin'."

The marshall climbed over the dirt pile and stepped back down on the street. Nathan noticed his strong arms, broad shoulders, and the dirt that covered him from hat to boot.

"Son, I need to wash up and grab my pistol. Now tell me the story about Marcus Dawson getting robbed."

Nathan reviewed the whole story, from his meeting with the man on the stage from Battle Mountain Station to hitching up with Mr. Dawson in the Shoshone village, to the robbery where the horse played dead, and the disaster with the wagon.

The marshall's office turned out to be an eight-by-eight-foot jail built of two-foot-thick timbers, with a dirt floor and with iron bars on the windows and doors.

Nathan watched him splash some water on his face, pull on a fresh shirt, and strap a long-barreled pistol on his hip.

The two of them walked over to the hotel and found Dr. Stryker resetting Marcus Dawson's broken legs. The old trader had not yet regained consciousness.

"Now, son, er . . . what was your name?" the marshall asked.

"Nathan T. Riggins of, well, I used to live in Indiana."

"Nathan, you said you could identify the man with the gold-triggered gun even though he had a mask over his face during the robbery, is that right?"

"Yes, I know it's him. I remember him from the stage."

"Well, most men don't like being accused of robbin' and stealin', so there might be a little tussle, if you know what I mean," Marshall Kholey reported.

"You mean a gunfight?" Nathan inquired.

"Now I'm not too sure about guns, but I'd like to play it safe. I want you to go around back of the Wild Horse and enter the kitchen. Tell Chico I sent you. Then move up to the doorway and watch the action. I'll start a conversation with the man and then look your way. If he's the one, just nod your head." The marshall put his hand on Nathan's shoulder. "Can you do that?"

Nathan froze for a moment, not because of fear, but because he just realized that it had been weeks since anyone had touched him.

I've got to find Mom and Dad soon!

"Son . . ." the marshall repeated, "can you do that?"

"Oh," Nathan stammered, "yes, sir! I'll do it."

He discovered that the backside of the Wild Horse Cafe was the backside of Galena. There was nothing beyond the building but holes in the ground, piles of dirt, and a few dirty tents. Inside he found a man he supposed to be Chico, explained his situation, and went over to stand by the kitchen door.

Fearing that the outlaw would recognize him, Nathan pushed the door open only a few inches. As it turned out, the outlaw's table was fairly close to the kitchen, and the man sat with his back against the wall where he could view the front entrance as well as the rear one. Nathan listened as the marshall approached the table from the front door and began a conversation.

"Afternoon. It's kind of crowded in here. Can I use part of your table?"

The man looked up slowly as if to size up the marshall's intent. "Yep. Be my guest."

"Old Chico fries up a mighty good pepper steak," the marshall added. "Say, that's one fine pistol you've got there. I haven't seen a gold trigger like that except for Gideon Shay down in Austin. You didn't buy that from Gideon, did you? He promised that if he ever sold it, I could buy it."

The man continued to finish eating his steak and mumbled through the bites, "Nope, I didn't get it in Austin. I've had this pistol for six years now. I don't intend on selling it either."

Marshall Kholey glanced over at Nathan, who was nodding his head.

"Well, I'm mighty sorry to hear that. I'm the marshall here, and I'll need to take you over to the jail for some questions about robbing Marcus Dawson." The marshall's hand rested lightly on the oak handle of his pistol.

"Marshall, where I come from, you don't go around accusing people of being outlaws unless you're ready to back it up." The man pushed his plate back, but kept his hands above the table.

"Just where is it you come from, and what is your name?" the marshall asked.

"The name's Lexie Devere from San Francisco, and I have no intention of answering any more questions!" Nathan saw the man push the table back and tilt back in the chair moving his hands slowly down to his side.

"Devere? Now I don't suppose you're related to Donovon Devere? We strung him up for horse theft over at Humboldt Wells last summer." The Marshall never took his eyes from Devere's gun hand.

Then, without warning, the outlaw went for his gun, and that very instant Marshall Kholey shoved the whole table into Devere, tipping over his chair and causing him to crash to the floor before he could get the gun out of the holster.

Devere could only look up at the marshall's drawn gun. "Riggins," the marshall called, "you can come out here now."

Nathan walked out into the dining room, and the men who had been eating dinner now gathered around.

"Is this the man?" Marshall Kholey asked Nathan.

"Yeah, he's the one. I recognized his gun and his voice and that dirty coat," Nathan nervously admitted.

The man on the floor looked over at Nathan, then up at the marshall. "You ain't going to take the word of no half-breed, are you?"

Nathan looked at Marshall Kholey. "Half-breed?" he questioned.

"With the moccasins and beaded shirt, I guess you look like a half-breed Indian," Marshall Kholey nodded.

"Even if I was, what difference does that make?" Nathan questioned.

"Not one bit to me," the marshall replied. "Come on, Devere, get up!"

"You ain't putting me in that jail," the man commanded.

"Well, boys," the marshall appealed to those standing around, "what should I do with this hombre that just bushwhacked Marcus Dawson?"

"He laid into old Marcus?" one of the men pressed.

"Sure did. Broke both his legs and no telling what else," the marshall reported.

"I say we hang him," the man offered.

Nathan heard men all through the crowd mumble the same thing.

"You see, Devere, you picked the wrong town to hide in. Most every man in this building has been outfitted by Dawson at one time and another. Lot of them owe their start to the old man's credit. So you either walk peacefully over to the jail, or I just walk out of here and let these boys take care of things."

"You wouldn't do that!" Devere pleaded.

"He's all yours, boys. Come on, Nathan, this could get ugly." The marshall nodded at Nathan.

"Wait! I'm coming, Marshall!" Devere cried out as he leaped to his feet and hurried across the room.

■

With Devere safely in jail, Marshall Kholey and Nathan walked over to the hotel to check on Marcus Dawson. They were surprised to see him propped up on a couple of cushions, fully alert.

The marshall smiled at Dr. Stryker and then turned to the injured trader. "Marcus, how are you doing?"

"I got two broken legs and pain from the tip of my toes to the top of my old gray head. I feel like a herd of buffalo just waltzed over the top of me. Other than that, I'm tolerable. Did you find your gold mine in the street?"

"By morning. We'll find her by morning," the marshall acknowledged. "Listen, the boy . . . Nathan, he brought you in and spotted the bushwhacker. Got him locked up now."

"Well, son," the old man said slowly and deliberately, "I owe you one. If you need something, you let me know. I might have lost my goods, but chances are my credit's good any place in town."

Nathan looked at the old man, then at the marshall. "Look, can I, eh, you know, borrow one of your horses to ride down to the Jersey district and look for my parents?"

"I'll say you can. But they're just plodders. You won't make very good time," Dawson added. "The horse you ought to use is the one that bushwhacker had. Did you see how he tricked us into thinking it was dead?"

Marshall Kholey entered the conversation. "Well, son, you take one of Dawson's drivin' horses. I can't get rid of Devere's horse until he faces trial. I'll have to send for the judge."

"Mr. Dawson's horse would be great!" Nathan blustered. "Maybe . . . is there any chance of getting some food to take on the journey? I guess I'm kind of broke. But I'll pay it back."

Marcus Dawson sighed deeply and lay back down on the cushions. "Marshall, I believe there was a ten dollar reward for that bushwhacker's capture, wasn't there?"

"Reward?" the marshall said in surprise. "Oh, yeah . . . he's right, son." Marshall Kholey walked over to a small table and took out a piece of paper upon which he scribbled a note. Then, turning to Nathan, he explained, "Just take this over to Galena Mercantile. They'll let you buy ten dollars worth of supplies."

"Thanks! And the horse, Mr. Dawson, I'll bring it right back as soon as I find my parents."

Marcus Dawson didn't open his eyes. "Son, you take good care of that animal. I won't need him for six weeks, seeing how I'm so busted up."

"Well," the marshall interrupted, "I'll need to see

you in about a week. That's as soon as the judge will make it up here. I'll need your testimony at the trial."

"Son," Dawson asked, "how's that dog of yours?"

"He's, you know, scared to come into town. So he's waiting out there in the sagebrush for me," Nathan reported.

"Smart dog," Dawson added. "You ride easy goin' down to Jersey."

"Yes, sir." Nathan nodded. "And thanks for the supplies!"

"You earned them, son." The marshall smiled.

■

Nathan hustled out of the hotel, crossed the dusty street, and scuffled toward the Galena Mercantile. He didn't notice anyone on the crowded street until someone caught the arm of his shirt.

He spun around. There was the barefoot girl.

"Hey! You aren't mad at me, are you?" she quizzed.

"Mad?"

"About the shoes. Really," she explained, "I liked those fancy shoes. It's just, you know, I ain't got no shoes." She brushed her long brown hair back on her shoulder. Nathan hadn't noticed her blue eyes before. "What's your name?" she asked.

"Ah, I'm Nathan T. Riggins of . . . eh, my name's Nathan."

"That's a Bible name, ain't it?" She smiled.

"Yeah, I suppose so." Nathan felt his usual awkwardness in speaking to girls.

"I got a Bible name," she smiled. Not waiting for his reply she continued, "I'm Leah, and she was Jacob's wife. Did you ever have the Bible read to you?"

Nathan turned and stepped toward the store with the girl by his side. "Certainly. I read the Bible. Everybody's read the Bible!"

"I cain't read." Leah looked down at her dirty long dress.

"It's not all that hard," Nathan shrugged, enjoying his own importance. "I could teach you sometime." The minute the words fell out of his mouth, he regretted his pride.

"Really? You'd teach me to read?" Leah giggled.

Nathan tried to bury the topic. "Sure, when I have time. But I've got to ride down to the Jersey mines and find my parents first."

"Have you got a horse?" Leah sounded surprised.

"Yes. Now I need some supplies." Nathan pushed open the door of the Galena Mercantile and held it open for Leah, who stared, then proudly walked through.

Once inside, Leah disappeared, and Nathan gathered supplies. Besides food, he purchased a new hat and hunting knife to replace the ones he had lost. Paying for his goods, he grabbed up the flour sack full of supplies and noticed that he had two dollars' worth of credit left over.

Walking toward the candy counter, he spotted Leah staring at a glass case.

"Do you want a candy stick?" he offered.

She didn't look in his direction. He walked over to her and realized that she was staring at a pair of black lace-up shoes.

Walking back to the clerk, Nathan asked, "How much money for those black lace-ups?"

"Two dollars, son, and that's a bargain rate. We just don't get a call for that small of a shoe."

"Listen, I'll use that last part of my credit for those shoes. Just give them to that girl at the case after I've left."

Nathan grabbed his grub sack and went out the front door leaving Leah still leaning on the case.

■

It only took a few minutes for Nathan to pick up Marcus Dawson's horse at the stables. The marshall had stopped by and left off an old saddle for him. Nathan rode the horse between the corral and the hotel and started to head south out of Galena when he remembered the dog.

Tona? Where's that dog?

He circled around the outside of Galena, whistling for the dog. After a while Tona silently showed up, trotting alongside the big horse. Nathan avoided going back up the street, out of respect for the dog. As he ambled along behind the buildings, his thoughts drifted to his sudden good fortune.

Lord, it's me, Nathan T. Riggins of . . . of Nevada. Thanks, Lord, for helping Mr. Dawson. I guess it was sort of Your plan that I was there to bring him in. Maybe, maybe all this isn't a big mistake. And thanks for this old horse and the food and everything.

"Hey!"

Nathan pulled up on the reins. He twisted in the saddle just as Leah ran up behind him.

"Look at my new shoes!" she shouted.

"They look very nice," Nathan said.

"Did you really buy them for me?" she asked.

"Well, sort of, I mean, there was this reward money, and I just didn't need it all, and . . . well, you—"

"Thank you very much," she said smiling. "But there's something I've got to tell you."

"What?" Nathan turned the horse towards Leah.

"I ain't ever going to marry nobody but Kylie Collins," she shouted.

Nathan shoved his new hat on the back of his head. He kicked the horse with both heels and trotted off towards the Jersey mining district.

8

*T*his was not the first time Nathan had left Galena, Nevada, to look for his parents. But this time definitely was different.

Sometimes days, weeks, even years seem to drag by without challenge or change. Some people call them peaceful. Some call them boring.

Then there are moments . . . if a person is fortunate, days and weeks . . . when life is lived with such excitement and challenge the person is, if he or she survives, forever changed.

These were days like that, and Nathan T. Riggins, formerly of Indiana, knew it.

This time he left town with a horse, whom he quickly named Ace.

This time he had supplies tied carefully behind his cantle.

This time he had a dog. Tona trotted far ahead of the horse.

And this time he felt respect, not hostility, for the barren land that stretched out ahead of him.

The hot summer sun baked Nathan's backside as he rode southeast across the Reese River Valley.

There were no farms.

No homes.

No barns.

No cattle.

No trees.

No people.

Just two dusty ruts winding their way through the sage towards some place called Jersey.

Ace was not the fastest horse Nathan had ridden. He was certainly not the most handsome. But years of pulling Marcus Dawson's wagon had taught the big black gelding how to keep a steady pace and never stop.

Nathan had plenty of time to think, and the first thing that came to his mind was how many things he didn't know.

I don't know how far it is to Jersey!

I don't know if this road leads all the way there.

I don't know if there's water along the route.

I don't know if there are Indians over here, too.

I don't even know if my parents are there.

The trail led him across the Reese River, and then it turned south. As the sun was setting, he saw that the wagon ruts forked, with one set running east toward a tall mountain still reflecting snow from its peak. The other trail led away from the river in a southeast direction. Nathan took the southeast trail, promising himself that he would stop and make camp at the first sign of some trees.

The sun had set, and Ace was still plodding along the trail when Nathan gave up looking for a pleasant spot to make camp. He caught sight of a small patch of ankle-deep green grass a few hundred feet from the trail. Further investigation revealed a bubbling spring that soaked an area about the size of a small corral.

He pulled the saddle off Ace, led him to the grass, and hobbled him for the night. Camp consisted of a tiny sage-wood fire, a saddle to lean against, and Tona, as always, watching from a distance.

Nathan tossed three short sticks on the fire and leaned against his saddle. It seemed to him that the stars dangled only a few feet above his head. Glancing at the Big Dipper, he drew an imaginary line up from Merak and Dubhe, the two front stars in the constellation, enabling him to locate the North Star.

He then drew a line in the dirt straight toward the North Star, tossed the stick in the fire also, and promptly went to sleep.

■

Morning in the high Nevada wilderness held a special quality for Nathan.

Everything always feels new! It's like the first day of creation or something. Maybe God spends all night repainting everything!

Ace stood in the middle of the pasture, nibbling on the grass and ignoring Tona, who was occupied with the scent of animals near the little spring. Nathan saddled the horse, ate a bite of breakfast, and was soon back on the southeast trail.

Way before the sun was straight above, Nathan felt

the wind shift. Instead of pushing him from behind, it now swirled around Ace and blasted straight into their faces. Not long after the change in the wind, he spotted a long dark cloud lining the entire southeastern horizon.

"Oh, great," Nathan spoke to Ace and Tona, "we're going to get rained on!"

The giant cloud rolled across the sky like leaves tumbling in the wind. Nathan watched with interest as the sickly brown, gray, yellow cloud raced towards him. It was different from anything he had ever experienced. There were no clouds above him and no heavy air ladened with moisture. Just that long unbroken cloud like a giant curtain falling across the southeastern sky.

Nathan fastened the stampede string of his hat securely under his chin and leaned into the wind that now picked up sand, dirt, and debris. Ace hung his head low and continued to plod. Through the swirling dust, Nathan noticed that Tona had pulled in close and now walked only a step or two ahead of the horse.

The sand pelted Nathan's face and hands, stinging with increasing pain every exposed skin surface.

This isn't rain! It's a sandstorm! Nathan groaned.

Within minutes the sky darkened into a swirling, biting, dark mass. Nathan closed his eyes, leaned down to the left side of the saddle horn, and tried to shield his face behind his hat and Ace's neck.

There was no way of telling if he was still on the wagon trail. Tona now walked right next to the stirrup by Nathan's left foot. Nathan could not see anything beyond the heads of his two traveling companions. Ace took small careful steps, and Nathan let the reins drop limp on the horse's neck.

This has got to blow past. It can't just go on and on. Lord, I didn't need this.

After a considerable time, Nathan realized that Ace had stopped moving forward and had turned completely around so that the sandstorm blasted them from the rear.

Nathan pulled his bandana from his pocket and tied it around his face, blocking some of the sand and dirt from entering his mouth. Then he slid from the saddle to the ground and, bringing the reins under Ace's neck, tied the leather straps to his left wrist. With eyes squinted nearly shut, he loosened the cinch on the saddle and then turned the horse back around to face the storm. Taking the lead, he pulled a reluctant Ace behind him. Nathan wished he had a leash to keep Tona close, but the dog didn't seem to be in the mood for wandering away.

I've got to find shelter. There has to be a tree, or some rocks, or a cave, or an old mine, or something! Lord, help me find something!

Nathan didn't see the upended wagon until he crashed into it. Ducking down behind the slats of the wagon bed, he found that it blocked much of the wind's force. He spun around and slid to a sitting position with his back leaning against the overturned wagon. He pulled Ace's head down behind the windbreak, and the black gelding kept his head tucked down next to Nathan's.

Pushing back his hat with his left hand, Nathan leaned his head into his knees and closed his eyes tight. Within a moment he felt the warm, furry body of Tona huddled against his moccasins. Without opening his eyes, he reached down and stroked the dog's back.

It was the first time Nathan had actually touched the dog.

Nathan fought to keep the sand out of his mouth, nose, eyes, and ears. He dozed in and out of consciousness. He wasn't sleepy, but the darkness and the drone of the storm lulled him into nodding off.

His sand-blasted eyes began to play tricks on him. Bright red flashes of light jumped at him—even when his eyes were closed. At one point he dreamed that he was on a high cliff looking down at some travelers far below. He knew it was his parents, but no matter how loud he yelled, he couldn't get their attention. In another dream he was being chased through the woods by an angry Lexie Devere. Then the red flashes appeared again, and Nathan tried to rub his eyes, but only succeeded in hurting himself even more.

He had no way of knowing how long he had been huddled up against the wagon. It seemed like hours.

It might be night. This just can't keep going; it's got to stop!

It was Ace raising his head and tugging on the reins tied to Nathan's hand that finally woke him. The storm had disappeared. The sun, low on the western horizon, sparkled on the loose sand that piled in a smooth sculpture around the old overturned wagon.

Nathan jerked the bandana down around his neck, pulled off his hat, and tried to shake the sand out of his hair. Brushing off his clothes, he climbed up on an exposed wagon wheel and surveyed the countryside. For miles all Nathan could see was sand. In the distance, which he supposed to be south, was a mountain range.

"Just rows and rows of sand dunes," Nathan reported to Ace. "The sagebrush is almost covered!"

He didn't see Tona anywhere, but soon discovered the dog's tracks leading away from the wagon. Having no better plan, Nathan followed Tona's trail out of the sand dunes. At first he attempted to walk out leading the horse. But after several halting, moccasin-filling steps, he tightened the cinch and climbed back aboard the horse.

The sandstorm had changed the landscape for several miles in every direction, but within a half hour, Nathan and Ace trudged out of the dunes and returned to the rolling sagebrush-covered hills of northern Nevada. He could not see Tona, but the dog's tracks were easy to spot in the windblown wilderness.

The wind, only a short time before violent and vicious, settled down to a mere whisper. Long prairie shadows made tracking more difficult, and when Nathan reached some granite outcroppings, he lost Tona's paw prints entirely. To Nathan's surprise, it was Ace that took over now. The big horse seemed to be driven by instinct as he skidded up the granite mountain, horseshoes clanging against the stone.

Halfway up the mountain, Nathan thought he could see Tona's silhouette on top of the rocky cliff. As he and Ace approached, the dog suddenly appeared, trotting alongside them in silence.

"Tona," Nathan called out, "why on earth did you lead us way up here?"

The dog didn't smile or respond. It was almost dark when Nathan crested the mountain and discovered a large pool of water filling a granite basin about the size of a schoolhouse.

"Tona! How did you know about this pool?" Nathan blurted out. He quickly slid off Ace and headed for the water. After he and Tona had a quick dip in the clear, cold water, Nathan made camp.

He knew it would not be a comfortable night. There was no wood or chips for a fire. No trees for protection from the wind. And no soft spot to call a bed. Nothing but cool water and hard rock.

The sky was clear, and the moon was bright when it poked its way into the darkness of the eastern horizon. Nathan leaned against his saddle and watched the stars and moon in silent reflection on the pool of water. Ace stood, hobbled, not more than ten feet from Nathan. He could see Tona keeping guard at the edge of the water.

Even though he sat upright, Nathan dozed in and out of sleep. Visions of Indians and outlaws, empty towns and crowded streets floated through his mind in no apparent order.

A sudden wild bark from Tona brought him to his feet, and a cold sweat broke out on his neck. Peering through the moonlight, he saw the dog lock his jaw right behind the head of the largest snake Nathan had ever seen. For a few seconds, the wiry gray and white dog violently shook the huge rattler and then slung it to its death on the rocks below the water.

Then Tona turned and limped toward Nathan, whining at every step.

"Tona! You got bit!" Nathan cried. "Tona!" The dog struggled right up to him and then flopped over on his side. Nathan could see the dog's labored breathing. Without hesitating, Nathan pulled the leather lacing out of his beaded shirt and tied it around Tona's snake-bitten left front leg. Taking his hunting knife, he cut an X across the snake bite. Tona opened his eyes wide but did not even whimper.

"What did Gwee-ya do for Eetahla? Oh, man . . . Tona, please don't die. . . . Hakinop! I need some hakinop. There isn't even sagebrush up here. Wait! Suck out the poison. Oakes told me you have to suck out the poison."

Nathan stared at the dog's bloody leg. "Lord, help me!" he mumbled. Then he sucked on the wound and spat on the ground.

"Ugh! Now I've got to find that root."

Working in the moonlight as quickly as possible, Nathan flung the saddle on Ace, jammed the bit in his mouth, tied the supplies on his back, and carefully laid Tona across the horse's withers.

With the North Star as a guide and moonlight to see by, Nathan guided Ace southeast off the rocky mountaintop.

Daylight broke when he reached a narrow strip of overgrowth alongside a tiny stream bed. He scrambled off

Ace, carried Tona to the water, and tried to get him to drink. Leaving the dog at the water's edge, Nathan raced along the stream bank searching for the carrotlike plant with long, white roots, the plant called hakinop by Gwee-ya.

Falling to his knees, Nathan dug wildly at the roots of a plant he thought was correct. He knew it would be too late to look for any other plant. Running back to Tona, he inspected the snake bite, which now had swollen the dog's leg to twice its original size.

As he mashed the hakinop, Nathan saw that Tona's eyes were closed; his tongue lay listless on the dirt as he struggled to breathe through his open mouth.

"Now look, Tona, you've got to get better. Listen, we've got a lot of things to do. You've got to understand, Tona. I need you to help me find my parents, and then we'll have a house and settle down, and you and I can go for hikes, and hunt, and play ball, and . . ."

Nathan fought to keep the tears from blocking his vision, "We can just sit on the porch and watch the sun go down . . . Lord, please don't let Tona die!"

Nathan used the clean bandana to wipe the tears from his eyes. Then he plastered the wound with mashed hakinop and wrapped it tight.

Tona's breathing now was so uneven that several times Nathan thought the dog had died.

After almost an hour of sitting beside the stream, Nathan got up and pulled the saddle from Ace and hobbled the horse near the water's edge. He checked on Tona, ate a couple slices of dried fruit, then leaned against his saddle, and fell asleep.

When Nathan woke up, the sun was straight above him and glared in his eyes. He splashed some water on his face and checked on Tona, who still labored with every breath. Nathan took some water in his hand and forced some into the dog's dry mouth. Then he carried the dog to a place in the shade.

A week ago I couldn't have cared less about this dog. Now it's like my whole life is waiting for him to pull through, or die. It doesn't make sense, Lord. I didn't even want a dog. I didn't ask for this mutt to follow me. It's all Your fault. If my folks had been there to meet me, none of this would have happened!

It was a long, hot, quiet afternoon. For the first time in a week, Nathan did not hurry to get somewhere. There was nothing to do but wait . . . watch Tona . . . nap . . . wait and pray . . . and check on the dog again.

About sundown, he noticed the first sign of improvement. Tona opened his left eye and stared at Nathan when he came to check on him. By nightfall, Tona had both eyes open, but still did not move nor make a sound. In checking the snakebite, Nathan discovered that Tona's leg was stiff as a stick. A quick examination revealed that all his legs were in the same locked position.

Nathan started holding each leg, one at a time, and exercising it, stretching the muscles, forcing it to bend. Tona winced only when Nathan flexed the bitten leg.

Building a small fire out of dry branches, Nathan

made camp for the night. He spent several minutes every hour exercising Tona's stiff joints.

Sometime in the dead of night, he struggled out from under his blanket to check on the dog and was startled to see light from a flickering campfire several hundred yards downstream.

Curious, he started slowly toward the fire. Nathan T. Riggins of Indiana would have barged right into that camp looking for someone to help with Tona. But Nathan T. Riggins of Nevada crept silently through the brush, settling down to listen as he inched closer to the two men sitting by the fire.

9

You figure we'll have to shoot it out in Galena?"

"If they ain't hung him already."

"But the judge don't get there until at least next Monday."

"Judge ain't the only one who hangs."

"You mean—"

"Sure, that old man was one of their own. Them miners stick up for each other."

"Well, so do we. Devere pulled us out of that scrape down in Gold Mill."

Devere? These men are going to help Lexie Devere?

Nathan hunkered down behind some bushes and continued to listen. He could see no faces, just the men's backs as they sat near the fire.

"You reckon we can get there by tomorrow night?"

"If we ride hard and the horses hold up and the trail hasn't blown full of sand and we get a little rest tonight."

With those words the men stretched out on their blankets and went to sleep. Nathan crept back to his campsite, checked on Tona, and then laid back down against his saddle.

"I've got to warn Marshall Kholey in Galena," Nathan mumbled in low, hushed tones, enjoying the sound of a voice, even if it was his own. "But I don't think I can find my way back from here, and there was so much sand."

Through the moonlit shadows he caught sight of Ace, who drooped his head in a sleepy posture.

Suddenly Nathan sat straight up.

Lord, if it's really Your providence that I was right here tonight, then I think You would want me to go back and warn the folks in Galena. So . . . that's what I'm going to do. Lord, I hope I know what I'm doing.

Saddling Ace in the dark, Nathan led the horse to the creek for a drink, and then went over to the resting Tona. Once again, he spread the barely breathing dog across the horse and pulled himself up into the saddle.

Scattered clouds had begun to blow in, and Nathan lost sight of the North Star, but he figured he could find north anyway.

Daylight came on the desert with the heavy black clouds of a summer storm hanging so low that Nathan could not see the mountains on the horizon, nor could he tell which direction was east. There simply was no rising sun.

Tona bounced along in front of the saddle with open eyes. Nathan kept rubbing each leg, bending and stretching them, trying to loosen the stiffened joints. The scenery looked familiar—draws with dried creek beds and rolling, sage-covered hills—and yet he wasn't sure.

Nathan had hoped to come to the sand dunes by

noon, but after hours of riding, he found neither sand nor noon. The storm did not drop a trace of rain, but continued to blanket the sun from view. Coming across a wagon rut that hadn't been used since the last rains, Nathan turned left towards some mountains that had now come into view.

"It's either a road into Galena or a road out of Galena," he told Tona. The dog didn't respond.

Only a few minutes down the trail, Nathan stopped the horse, rubbed his eyes, and stared at an object not more than twenty feet away from the wagon rut.

"A piano? An upright piano out in the middle of nowhere?" he muttered.

Crawling off Ace, he led the horse over to the dust-covered piano that sat majestic among the sage. The weathered wood told Nathan that it had been here for a long time. Lifting up the lid, he struck several notes and was not surprised to find there was no sound. Checking out the back, he discovered that the frame, hammers, and wire had all been gutted out.

"It's only a shell," he announced to his animal companions.

The backside of the piano had been carved up with names. At the head of the list were the words, "Giles family— August 1867—it can't get any worse than this!" Underneath, in a different writing style Nathan spotted, "It got worse."

He sat on the piano and ate dinner. Then he started back along the wagon ruts. At midafternoon the sun finally broke through the clouds, and it horrified Nathan.

"The sun's over there?" he shouted. "Then I'm going south instead of north! I'm further away from Galena than ever before!"

Looking up at the mountain, he spotted a coil of dust from a horse and rider coming towards him. Nathan looked for a place to hide, but the low sagebrush offered no cover. So he rode towards the rider, who turned out to be a thin man with a wispy goatee.

The man drew up on the reins, pulled his pistol out of the holster, and looked at Nathan.

"You speak English?" he asked.

"Of course," Nathan shrugged. "Is this the Galena road?"

"Yep. You ain't an Indian?"

"No, I just got these moccasins and shirt for a present, that's all."

"Is that dog dead?" he asked.

"No," Nathan assured him. "He's been snake-bit."

"You going to eat him?"

"What?" Nathan gasped.

"I hear they make awful good stew." The man smiled, showing that his upper front teeth were missing.

"How much further up this hill to Galena?" Nathan changed the subject.

"Up the hill? You can ride until Christmas, and you won't get to Galena up there."

"But," Nathan protested, "you said this was the way to Galena!"

"Nope," the man answered, "I said this is the

Galena Road. I'm going toward Galena; you're headed to Jersey."

"Jersey? How far is it?"

"Two, maybe three miles. Just over that pass." He motioned with his arm.

"Are you going straight to Galena?" Nathan quizzed.

"Yep. Need some supplies."

"Do you know Marshall Kholey?"

"Sure, don't everybody?"

Nathan took a deep breath. "Listen, can you give the marshall an important message? Tell him some men are going to try to break Lexie Devere out of jail. I overheard them talking, and I wanted to warn the marshall. But if I'm only a few miles from Jersey, I've got to look for my parents. You don't happen to know David and Adele Riggins, do you?"

"Sorry, son, I've never heard of them. But don't you worry, I'll talk to the marshall." The man rode off in a wild gallop.

As Nathan watched him go, he rubbed Tona's legs. "Well, we stumbled into Jersey, Tona."

Remembering the man's comments about the way he looked, Nathan poured a little water from his canteen on his bandana and tried to wipe off his dusty face.

"My mother will pitch a fit if she sees me this dirty," Nathan explained to Tona and Ace. He felt a little cleaner, but he could tell he had caked dirt on his neck and shoulders.

He felt a surge of nervous excitement as he crested

the mountain. The sun had broken through the clouds, sending streams of light onto the mountain slope below.

"Where's the town?" Nathan groaned. Stretched out far below him was a mountainside full of men digging holes and sifting dirt. He thought he spotted a white tent or two, but he couldn't see any buildings at all.

A few miles down the trail, he came upon two men digging wildly in the yellow-red dirt.

"Excuse me, eh . . . sir, I'm looking for my parents, David and Adele Riggins. Have you seen them?"

"Diggin's? Get your own diggin's!" one man shouted.

"No, I'm looking for my father—David Riggins."

"What?" The other man stopped shoveling and looked at his partner.

"He lost his diggin's," the first man replied without stopping.

"Sorry to hear that, son." The man nodded at Nathan and wiped his brow. "Is your dog dead?"

"No," Nathan sighed. "Where's town?"

"What town?"

"Jersey, Nevada," Nathan said.

"This is it."

Nathan looked around at the miners on the hillside. "Where?"

"Right here. Why this just might be the main street someday."

"You mean, there aren't any buildings?" Nathan quizzed.

"What for? Hope you find your diggin's," the man replied and returned to his work.

Just down the trail Nathan came across a small tunnel dug back into the mountain. He dismounted, led Ace toward the tunnel entrance, and peered in. Soon a white-bearded man emerged pushing a wheelbarrow full of rocks and dirt.

"Excuse me, I'm looking for David and Adele Riggins. Have you seen them?" Nathan questioned.

The old man paused, looked hard at Nathan, then shrugged, and went on. Nathan followed him down the hill until he dumped the load.

"Have you seen my father, David Riggins?" Nathan demanded.

The man shrugged again. "No English, no talk English," he stammered with a heavy accent.

"You don't speak English?"

The man shook his head.

"Does anyone in the tunnel," Nathan asked as he motioned, "speak English?"

The man paused. Then he spotted Tona lying across Nathan's horse.

"Dog dead?"

"No! The dog's not dead!" Nathan sighed in disgust.

Several hundred yards downhill, he came upon six men standing in a circle arguing loudly.

". . . and if we catch you digging close to our claim, you'll never see your Mary again," one man shouted.

"Your claim? Your claim? You're getting crazy from

drinking the water," a man shouted back. "If this is your claim, what's its name?"

"It's the, ah, the . . ." The man spun around toward where Nathan was sitting on his horse. "It's the Dead Dog Mine, that's what it is!" he shouted.

"The dog's not dead!" Nathan corrected. But the argument continued without another glance at him.

Nathan heel-kicked Ace and rode around a bend in the road to find a near-white tent flapping in the breeze. In front of it an old door stretched across two barrels made a crude table or counter. Scrawled on the tent was the word *Store*.

"Excuse me," he called. "Anybody home?"

A voice boomed out of the tent, "We're closed!"

"Closed? It's the middle of the day," Nathan protested.

"Don't matter. We don't have anything left to sell!"

Nathan slid off Ace and walked over to the tent. "Do you happen to know David and Adele Riggins? I'm looking for them."

Nathan peeked into the tent and was startled to see a giant hole being dug right where the floor of the tent should have been. A huge man swung a pick, trying to dislodge some rocks below. "What are you doing?" Nathan asked.

"Diggin' for gold, just like everyone else," the man barked.

"Have you seen—"

"No, I haven't seen any Tiggins."

"Riggins," Nathan corrected.

"Them neither." The man crawled up out of the hole and came outside the tent. "Did you come down here from Galena?"

"Yes, sort of. I mean, I started out from Galena but got lost in a sandstorm," Nathan admitted.

"Did you see a freight wagon of goods headed this way driven by a man with a big white hat?"

"Eh, no," answered Nathan. "Are the goods for your store?"

"Providing I don't strike color first!" the man snorted. "Is that your horse?"

"I borrowed it from a friend," Nathan admitted.

"Is that dog dead?" the man asked.

"No!" Nathan shouted. He left the man standing by his tent and walked Ace on down the hill. Finding a scrap of canvas, Nathan picked up one of the red rocks dug out of the side of the mountain and used it to write on the canvas, "This dog is not dead!" Then he searched the ground near a broken wagon and found a horseshoe nail. Using the nail, he pinned the sign on Ace's saddle blanket right near Tona's head.

Nathan sighted another tent across the dry stream bed and scurried along in that direction. Arriving at the tent site, he noticed an area about the size of a small yard roped off in front of the tent. A sign warned, "Keep Out!" Two women dressed in long, black dresses sat guarding the tent with repeating rifles in their laps.

"Excuse me, ladies," he called from a safe distance.

"Keep moving, boy!" one woman called.

"What are you guarding?" he asked.

"Our claim. We'll be posted right here until Twyla gets back from filing papers."

"Oh, you ladies have a gold mine?"

"Who told you that?" the other woman shouted.

"Listen, did you by any chance meet my mother? Her name is Adele Riggins, originally from Indiana."

"We don't know any Adeles, but we heard there's a woman up by Lone Pine," one woman spoke up. "You might try up there."

"Lone Pine?" Nathan asked, "Is that a town?"

"The boy's not too bright, is he?" the other woman added. Then waving her rifle like a pointing stick, she said, "See that tree over on that eastern slope?"

"Yes." Nathan nodded.

"Well, it's a pine tree. Now do you see any other trees around it?"

"Eh, no," Nathan replied.

"Now you're catching on—lone pine. Go ask those digging by the pine."

Nathan mounted Ace and trotted toward the pine, holding Tona steady with his free hand.

Lord, this would be a good time to find my mom and dad!

There were so many miners digging around the pine that he couldn't ride the horse very close to the tree. Finally, he tied Ace to a large sage and carefully threaded his way between the dig holes and the hopeful prospectors.

He scanned each face for his mother or father.

This part of Nevada's high basin was crammed with people, but Nathan felt as alone as he had been in the wilderness. For almost an hour he went from person to person asking about his parents.

Finally, he thought he recognized a familiar face at the bottom of a deep, narrow pit. "Mr. Mallory! Mr. Mallory, is that you down there?"

"Who wants to know," boomed the voice.

"This is Nathan T. Riggins. I used to live in Indiana, and I rode on your stage last week."

"Riggins? Sure, kid, I remember. I'll be right up."

Climbing up out of the shaft, Mallory dusted off his trousers and pushed back his hat.

He took a careful look at Nathan. "Son, I hardly would have recognized you. So you finally caught up with your mom and dad. Now that's a good thing."

"No!" Nathan almost yelled. "I haven't found them."

"Well, I sent them to Willow Creek."

"You what?" Nathan's heart pounded. "You saw my parents?"

"I brought the stage down here last week and decided to quit and do a little digging myself. About the second or third day, I ran across your mother and father. Recognizing the name, I told them you were up at Willow Creek. Why, they left four days ago to go and find you."

"You really talked to my parents?" Nathan took a very deep breath and tried not to cry. "You sent them to Willow Creek?"

"Didn't you see them on the trail down?"

"No! I didn't see them. I was in a sandstorm, and I got lost, and Tona got snake-bit, and—"

"Well, if I were you, I'd head down that main road to Galena and just wait it out there. Sooner or later, they'll come by."

Nathan scanned the horizon. "Which is the main road?"

"Take the road north of that first draw, and then keep to the right. It will take you to Galena," Mallory instructed.

"Thank you!" Nathan called out as he turned to scamper down to Ace.

Willow Creek? There's nothing at Willow Creek!

10

*F*or the very first time since Nathan started west, he knew for sure that his parents were alive, close by, and looking for him. That news drove him from the Jersey mining district and along the main road back to Galena, even though it was almost dark. Stopping to rest only as needed, Nathan plodded down the trail past prospectors, supply wagons, and curiosity seekers headed for the rush.

Tona was regaining strength and could now use his front legs fairly well, but he had to drag both hind legs. Nathan let him continue to ride on Ace and was surprised how peaceful the restless dog had become.

About noon the next day, Nathan began to recognize the hillsides around Galena. Big Belle Mountain came into view, and the wind blew the sky clear. Cresting one of the mountain ridges, he stopped the horse, pulled off his hat, and scratched his neck.

"Something's wrong here," he muttered.

Below him on the far side of the mountain stood the familiar buildings and tents of Galena. But right down in the hollow, where Galena had been three days before, there was a crude fence around what had been the main street. Nathan could see several armed men patrolling on the inside of the fence.

"They moved the town! They moved a whole town in three days!" Nathan shouted to Ace and Tona.

Riding past the guarded area, Nathan approached town at a trot. Tona jumped off Ace's back and dragged himself around behind the buildings. Knowing that even while wounded, Tona could take care of himself, Nathan tied Ace to the porch post of the Galena Mercantile and banged his way through the front door.

The shelves of the store were only half full, and several clerks were busy with customers. Without waiting his turn, Nathan blurted out, "Has anybody here seen my parents?"

Those in the store stopped and turned toward Nathan, then went on about their business.

"Look, I need to find my father and mother, David and Adele Riggins. Has anyone seen them? They're looking for me."

"Son, we don't know anything about your parents. Now if you aren't buying something, just head on home!" a clerk insisted.

Home? I haven't been "home" in months!

Nathan searched the street in front of the store, and then plowed into the next building, which happened to be a tent-topped cafe. Rushing from table to rustic table, he saw that his parents were not there.

Within a half an hour, Nathan had surveyed almost every building and street in town. His parents were just not in Galena.

Nor was Marshall Kholey.

Nor was the marshall's office and jail.

In fact, no one looked familiar at all. It was as if he had stumbled into the wrong town.

He sat on the Mercantile steps next to Ace and stared out at the busy street crowded with strangers.

"It's like a play where people just say their lines and then walk off the stage," Nathan complained to Ace.

Lord, it's me, Nathan T. Riggins. I'm really tired. I'm tired of hurrying and getting nowhere. I'm tired of not getting enough sleep. I'm tired of being dirty. I'm tired of worrying night and day.

"Hey! What's that sign mean?"

Nathan looked up to see Leah standing by Ace looking at the sign "This dog is not dead!" still pinned to his saddle blanket.

"Leah! What happened around here?"

"Is your dog dead?" she asked.

"No!" he shouted. He jumped up and yanked down the canvas sign. It blew across the street and lodged against a wagon wheel.

"Leah, why did they move Galena?"

"Cause of the Shiloh, that's why," she said smiling.

"Shiloh?" Nathan asked.

"Yeah, the Shiloh Mine. Marshall Kholey and those other fellas hit color three days ago, right after you left town. So folks all staked out claims to the street, and yesterday they just drug all the buildings over here."

"They moved a whole town?"

Leah sat down on the steps and pulled up her long

dress so the black high-tops could be seen. "Nice shoes, huh?"

"Did you see my parents? They came back here to look for me, and now I can't find them," Nathan prodded.

"Maybe I seen 'em, maybe I didn't," Leah answered.

"What do you mean? Did you see them or not?" Nathan shouted.

"Well, I don't have to talk to no one who shouts at me," she pouted.

"Leah," Nathan said, fighting to hold back the tears, "I want to find my mother and father. Please, have you seen them?"

"Well, like I said, maybe I did. There's been new people in town everyday, and I've been out here on the street watching most all of them. But how would I know which is your kin? What did they look like?"

The question caught Nathan by surprise. "Look like? Well, my mother is sort of short, about my height . . . but maybe I'm taller than her now. Anyway, she has brown hair, but it was getting a little gray. And she wears . . ." Nathan grasped for the right words. "I don't have any idea what she would be wearing."

"Is your dad tall and thin, with a brown and gray beard?" Leah asked.

"No, he's big and strong—unless he's lost some weight. And he doesn't have a beard, anyway he didn't. He's got gray, narrow eyes that just sort of burn into you if you get him riled up."

"Well, I think maybe I seen 'em yesterday," Leah

offered. "There was this couple who came in from Jersey. I remembered it because there ain't many folks coming to town from that direction. And there ain't many women in town, especially ones who straddle a horse."

"My mom doesn't ride horses. She hates horses," Nathan stated.

"All I'm saying is that they came in from Jersey and asked me where the marshall was."

"The marshall! Marshall Kholey will know where they are. Where's his office now?"

"Don't got one." Leah shrugged.

"What do you mean? Of course, he's got an office. I was in it the other day when he locked up Lexie Devere," Nathan insisted.

"You been gone a long time. We don't got no jail, and we don't got no marshall, and we don't got no Lexie Devere."

"What?"

"The other day when the marshall struck gold in the street pit, he resigned and went to Austin to file a claim."

Nathan sat down next to Leah. "No marshall? What about Devere? Who's going to hold him over for trial?"

"Nobody, I guess," Leah replied. "Last night someone came to town and pulled over the jail. Lexie Devere escaped."

"Pulled over the jail?" Nathan asked.

"Yep. They just put ropes on the top, yanked it over on its side, and Devere walked out the bottom. That's it over there by the barber shop. I think they're going to just leave it on its side and make a saloon out of it."

"Devere's escaped! What about Marcus Dawson?" Nathan pressed.

"Oh, Mr. Dawson was put on a stage to Virginia City. And Devere is around town someplace. I heard he might be hiding out at the Lucky Strike Casino."

"He's in town? A criminal just wandering around?" Nathan stood up and stared down the street.

"Ain't got no marshall or jail. I guess no one wants to face him head on," Leah sighed. "Who was you talkin' to when I walked up?"

"What do you mean?"

"When I first come up behind you, you was talking to someone, but I couldn't see nobody," she said.

"Oh . . . I guess I was just sort of praying, you know."

"You were talking to God?" she continued to probe.

"Sure. Doesn't everybody?" He stood up again and scanned the street.

"I don't," Leah admitted. "I mean, nobody ever taught me how."

Nathan turned to look Leah in the eyes for the first time since she had walked up.

"You washed your face," he remarked.

"You didn't," she giggled.

"Isn't there a church in Galena?"

"No school, no church, and now no jail."

"I just can't believe that they would let Devere waltz around town."

"You could teach me." Leah squinted her eyes in the bright sunlight.

"Teach you what?"

Nathan realized that he had absolutely no idea what to do next, except that Mr. Mallory had suggested that he wait in Galena.

"You know, how to pray. I can learn things fast," Leah bragged.

Nathan hardly heard Leah's request.

Maybe that wasn't really my parents in Jersey. Maybe they got lost coming up here. Maybe they got bushwhacked. Or since the marshall wasn't here to tell them not to, they must have gone to Willow Creek.

That's it.

"Will you teach me?" Leah insisted.

"To pray?" Nathan replied, annoyed more than he wanted to admit.

"Yes."

"You don't need a teacher. Just talk to God like any important person, that's all."

Nathan unhitched Ace and started to walk the horse down the street. "I just can't believe they moved the whole town!"

Leah raced to keep up. "You mean like this, 'Mr. God, this is Leah, not the one in the Bible, but the one in Nevada, and I would sure be pleased if you would help Nathan find his mother and father. Thank You very much.'" At this point Leah held her dress and curtseyed. "Is that it? Did I do it right?"

Nathan took a deep breath and pushed his hat back.

"Yeah, that's all you need to do. Thanks for praying for me."

"You're welcome." Leah smiled. "Where are you going?"

"I was thinking about riding up to Willow Creek, but that's how I started all this. If they went up there, then they will come back here. So I'm just going to put the horse in the corral and wait for them."

A man wearing a full-length dress coat and mounted on a tall, black horse rode up to the corrals just as Nathan closed the gate.

"Son, give Cash a good rubdown and a few oats. I'll settle up with your boss later," he ordered as he dismounted. "Did they move town again?"

"Again?" Nathan mumbled.

"Well, take the horse," the man insisted.

"He don't work here, Judge," Leah interrupted.

"Judge? Are you the judge coming in for the hearing about Lexie Devere?"

"Sure am. Dewitt C. McKenney, Judge of the Fifth District," the man added. "Is anybody working at these corrals?"

"Nope," Leah answered, "they done quit to dig for gold down at Jersey. But my daddy says they'll be back as soon as they hear about the Shiloh."

"Well, I'll give you two bits if you'll put up this horse for me," the man offered.

"Ain't no use you staying in town." She shrugged.

"Yeah," Nathan added, "the marshall's quit, and Devere broke out of jail."

"Marshall Kholey quit? Devere's on the streets? I rode two hard days for this?" The judge sighed. "Well, I'll go check this out."

After caring for the judge's horse, Nathan and Leah closed the corral gate. Nathan climbed up to the top rail to look up the road toward Willow Creek. He thought he saw some riders headed for town. "I can't believe a guy like Devere is just walking around town!" Nathan complained still looking at the approaching riders.

One of those could be a woman, if she straddled up!

"I think I should go tell the judge what I know about Devere."

Nathan spun on the fence rail to jump down, but he was stopped by a face-to-face scowl from a big man holding a drawn pistol.

"Devere!" Nathan stammered.

Lexie Devere grabbed Nathan's beaded leather shirt, lifted him off the fence, and shoved him to the ground. Nathan's head spun with fear. He thought he heard some riders; he thought he heard Leah scream. He knew he had hit his head on something hard.

Without thinking, Nathan grabbed a handful of dirt and threw it at Devere, yelling, "Leah, run get the judge! Run get the judge." He rolled in the dirt to escape a wild kick from the outlaw; then suddenly Devere threw his hands up. Through the dust, Nathan saw a man with a rifle standing behind Lexie Devere.

The voice caught Nathan by surprise.

"Mister, I don't know who you are, and I don't know that Indian boy, but in my book no man treats a boy that way. Holster that gun. Do you hear me?" the man commanded.

Devere slowly returned the gold-triggered pistol to its holster. As if someone had just rolled back the clouds on a dark, dingy day, Nathan finally recognized the voice.

"Father!" Nathan shouted and scrambled to his feet. "It's me—Nathan. Daddy, it's really me! Daddy, I'm scared," Nathan sobbed. "I've been scared for a long time!" Nathan could feel giant tears plowing through the dirt on his face.

"Nathan?" The man's tone of voice softened.

As his father reached to help Nathan to his feet, Devere shoved him to the ground next to the boy and drew his gun out of the holster. Just as his hand cleared leather, Nathan saw an animal come flying out from behind a corral fence post.

"Tona!" he shouted.

Panicked by the dog on his arm, Devere shot wild and flung the dog to the ground. Instantly the outlaw swung the pistol to shoot the dog, but from behind him a rider on a horse plowed right into Devere, knocking him to the ground. Nathan's father quickly laid the barrel of his rifle against Devere's neck.

"Mister, I hope you've got things right with the Lord." Mr. Riggins didn't have any slack in his voice.

"Nathan!" a woman's voice called from horseback.

Suddenly, the woman who had run over Devere swung down out of the saddle and ran toward Nathan.

"Momma, I don't want to cry," Nathan sobbed. "Momma, I couldn't stay in Indiana another day.

Grandma and Grandpa died with the pox, and I've been looking for you for a long time!"

Nathan looked through the tears and felt his mother's arms around him. Nothing in his whole life had ever felt so good.

It might have been only a minute or two, or an hour, Nathan couldn't tell and didn't care. But then he heard some other voices.

"Sir, I'm Judge McKenney. If you'll take care of your family, we'll take care of Lexie Devere."

Nathan looked up to see several armed men surrounding them. Leah stood by the judge.

"What are you going to do with him?" Leah asked.

"We're taking him to Battle Mountain Station on the next stage and shipping him to Carson City." The judge pulled Devere to his feet and marched him back towards town.

■

Nathan's grandfather used to say that you could tell if a day was going to be a good one during the first ten minutes after you woke up.

Nathan had known all morning that this was a good one. Yesterday afternoon he had finally found his parents. Last night he had had a hot bath for the first time in a month. Then he got to sleep all night on a real bed at the hotel. He and his mother ate breakfast in the cafe—eggs, back bacon, and fresh buttered sweetbread.

Now he sat with his mother on a bench in front of

the hotel, waiting for his dad to return from a long meeting with Judge McKenney and some city leaders. Tona, who could now walk on his hind legs as well as ever, sat in the dirt at the far end of the hotel in a narrow alley that ran on the north side of the building.

"Hi!" Leah called, waiting for a stagecoach to pass by before she crossed the street. "Good morning, Nathan. Good morning, ma'am." She curtseyed.

"Well, good morning, Leah," Mrs. Riggins replied. "I do believe you scrubbed up last night."

"Yes, ma'am. So did Nathan, didn't he?" Leah smiled.

"Yes, but he insisted on wearing the beaded shirt and moccasins again," Mrs. Riggins added.

"I got new shoes," Leah beamed. "Nathan bought them for me!"

"He did?"

"Well, see, Mother," he said, a little embarrassed, "I had some credit that I didn't need, and I . . . well, Leah didn't have any shoes, and I thought it was the right thing to do."

Suddenly, Nathan saw Judge McKenney and two other men lead a shackled Lexie Devere over to the stage. Everyone on the front porch of the hotel walked over to view the proceedings.

"Wait a minute!" someone down the street shouted. A short, bald man with a handlebar moustache hustled up to the stage carrying something in his hand. "Seems like providence this sign was lying in the street this morning."

Lexie Devere left Galena with the sign "This dog is not dead!" tucked into his coat pocket.

"Dad, why were you gone all morning?" Nathan asked as his father returned to the hotel.

"Well . . . I guess I've got a new job," he announced.

"You mean we aren't going back to the Jersey district to strike it rich in a gold mine?" Nathan pressed.

"I guess not, son. Yesterday sort of reminded me that there are some things more important than gold."

Nathan's mother spoke up, "Like family?"

"Yeah, family, and law, and justice. I told them I'd take the job."

"What job?" Nathan asked.

"Marshall of Galena. What do you think, Nate?"

"You mean we get to live right here?"

Leah poked her head into the conversation. "Either right here, or down there, or over against Big Belle—who knows where they will move town next?" They all laughed.

"Well, Nathan Timothy," his mother added, "what do you think about that?"

"I think it's providence," he proclaimed.

"Providence?" His mother tilted her head as she spoke.

"Yeah. It's a matter of timing. God's really been in control all along, hasn't He?" Nathan nodded.

Mrs. Riggins ran her hand through Nathan's hair. "You're right. It is a matter of timing. We left you in Indiana because we didn't think you would be able to handle life out west. But you certainly seem to be ready for it now."

"And I didn't want to send for you," Nathan's father added, "until we could settle down in a real town. Now's the time for that, too."

"And it all happened," Nathan continued, "because you weren't here to meet me. That's what I mean, it must be God's providence."

"Sounds like you've learned quite a bit over the past weeks," his mother observed.

"I tell you one other thing I learned. I learned that there are some dogs that just don't smile." Nathan laughed.

"Look at Tona," Leah called. "He's smiling now!"

"That's not a smile," Nathan insisted.

"It is too!" she whined.

"That is not a smile."

"Nathan T. Riggins, Tona is smiling, and you just won't admit it," Leah harped.

"Listen, Tona is my dog. And I say that the dog is not smiling. Do you understand?" he shouted.

"Yeah, I understand," Leah pouted. "That's why I ain't ever going to marry nobody but Kylie Collins."

The conversation ended when a stagecoach pulled up in front of the hotel. Nathan spotted a boy about his age among the passengers. Walking over to the boy, he took in the crumpled eastern suit, tie, and slick, store-bought shoes.

"What are you staring at?" the boy barked at Nathan.

"Oh," Nathan said, clearing his voice, "nothing, really. I mean, I guess I was looking at your shoes."

"They happen to be the latest style in Chicago," the boy informed him. "I don't suppose you've ever been there. Well, my father is going to open a bank in this wretched place, so I suppose we will have to live here for a while."

Nathan grabbed the boy's arm. "Say, your name isn't Kylie Collins, is it?"

"Certainly not. I'm Colin Maddison, Jr. That's with two *d*'s," he lectured, pulling his arm back and entering the hotel.

Leah came up to Nathan's side. "He's rather strange, ain't he?"

"Give him time," Nathan replied. "It's surprising how much the West can change you in just one week."

Nathan walked across the street down in front of the newspaper office.

Maybe I should get a job at the newspaper. No, they need help at the livery. I'll work there until I save enough to buy a horse, and then . . . I guess I'll just wait and see.

For the first time in months, Nathan T. Riggins felt at home.